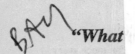 **"What**

Cameron asked her.

Draping an arm around Patricia's shoulders, Cameron drew her close to him. His sinewy strength was both solid and gentle.

"Everything...." The word came out half whisper, half sob.

"It can't be as bad as all that. Why don't you let me take a turn with the kids, and you can take a long walk."

Cameron found himself wondering what kind of man Patricia's late husband had been. He was inclined to believe the lout had never so much as lifted a finger to help out. It was a shock to discover that behind that superwoman mask was a vulnerable little girl. Cameron felt a fierce possessiveness well up inside him, to safeguard her against the world.

And the intensity of that feeling hit this confirmed bachelor like a ton of bricks....

Dear Reader,

The wonder of a Silhouette Romance is that it can touch *every* woman's heart. Check out this month's offerings—and prepare to be swept away!

A woman wild about kids winds up tutoring a single dad in the art of parenthood in *Babies, Rattles and Cribs... Oh, My!* It's this month's BUNDLES OF JOY title from Leanna Wilson. When a Cinderella-esque waitress—complete with wicked stepfamily!—finds herself in danger, she hires a bodyguard whose idea of protection means making her his *Glass Slipper Bride,* another unforgettable tale from Arlene James. Pair one highly independent woman and one overly protective lawman and what do you have? The prelude to *The Marriage Beat,* Doreen Roberts's sparkling new Romance with a HE'S MY HERO cop.

WRANGLERS & LACE is a theme-based promotion highlighting classic Western stories. July's offering, Cathleen Galitz's *Wyoming Born & Bred,* features an ex-rodeo champion bent on reclaiming his family's homestead who instead discovers that home is with the stubborn new owner...and her three charming children! A long-lost twin, a runaway bride...and *A Gift for the Groom*—don't miss this conclusion to Sally Carleen's delightful duo ON THE WAY TO A WEDDING.... And a man-shy single mom takes a chance and follows *The Way to a Cowboy's Heart* in this emotional heart-tugger from rising star Teresa Southwick.

Enjoy this month's selections, and make sure to drop me a line about *why* you keep coming back to Romance. We want to fulfill *your* dreams!

Happy reading,

Mary-Theresa Hussey

Mary-Theresa Hussey
Senior Editor, Silhouette Romance
300 East 42nd Street, 6th Floor
New York, NY 10017

Please address questions and book requests to:
Silhouette Reader Service
U.S.: 3010 Walden Ave., P.O. Box 1325, Buffalo, NY 14269
Canadian: P.O. Box 609, Fort Erie, Ont. L2A 5X3

WYOMING BORN & BRED

Cathleen Galitz

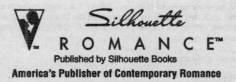

Silhouette
R O M A N C E™
Published by Silhouette Books
America's Publisher of Contemporary Romance

To the Miracle Two,
Shawn and Curt,
constant reminders of God's love
and blessings in my life.

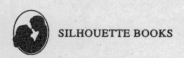

SILHOUETTE BOOKS

ISBN 0-373-19381-5

WYOMING BORN & BRED

Copyright © 1999 by Cathleen Galitz

This edition published by arrangement with Harlequin Books S.A.

® and TM are trademarks of Harlequin Books S.A., used under license. Trademarks indicated with ® are registered in the United States Patent and Trademark Office, the Canadian Trade Marks Office and in other countries.

Visit us at www.romance.net

Printed in U.S.A.

Books by Cathleen Galitz

Silhouette Romance

The Cowboy Who Broke the Mold #1257
100% Pure Cowboy #1279
Wyoming Born & Bred #1381

CATHLEEN GALITZ,

a Wyoming native, teaches English to seventh to twelfth graders in a rural school that houses kindergartners and seniors in the same building. She lives in a small Wyoming town with her husband and two children. When she's not busy writing, teaching or working with her Cub Scout den, she can most often be found hiking or snowmobiling in the Wind River Mountains.

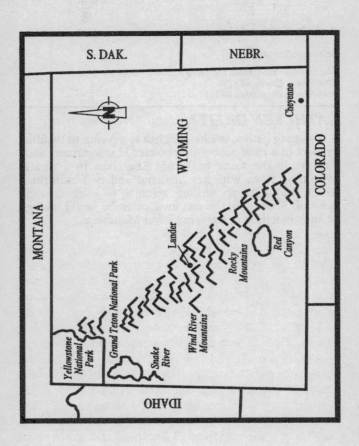

Chapter One

A cloud of dust as thick as regret dogged Cameron
Wade's pickup all the way down the washboardy road
leading him home. The hand carved sign that had once
so proudly heralded the Triple R was gone, but it came
as no surprise to him that the great knotty-pine archway
he had helped his father erect so many years ago still
stood silent sentry to the ranch where he had grown up.

As Cameron pulled into the driveway, he switched
off the sad song that Clint Black was warbling over the
airwaves. Precious little appeared to have been done
with the old place since the previous owner's death, but
he wasted little time contemplating the sad state of his
childhood home. He focused his attention instead upon
a balding spot of grass where two little boys were engaged in a game of cowboys and Indians, an integral
part of which appeared to be a toddler unhappily con-
strained in a playpen. As the boys whooped around their
makeshift stockade, their prisoner struck out at them
with a half-empty bottle. Diverted from their sport by

Cameron's unexpected presence, one of the urchins stopped long enough to holler out, "Hey there, mister."

Cameron gave the boy a cursory nod as he got out of his truck and made his way to the front door, frowning at the thought of having to knock to gain entrance to his old home.

"Watch out below!" warned a voice from above.

Cameron jumped aside just in time to avoid being hit by a large piece of shingling which rocketed off the roof and hit the ground beside him with a dull *thwack*. Squinting against the late-afternoon sun, he saw a teenager in a baseball cap and baggy overalls peering down at him from over the edge of the roof. The youth acknowledged him with a terse wave of the hand and a quick, sheepish grin.

"Sorry about that!" he called out. "Give me a minute and I'll be right down."

Tottering precariously close to the lip of the sharply peaked roof, the lad pitched an armload of shingles into the back of a rusty old pickup parked below, then proceeded cautiously toward a ladder propped against the house. Cameron hurried over to lend a steadying hand. An instant later he heard the crack of dry wood snapping just above his head.

A shrill scream pierced the sky as he reached out to catch the boy in midair.

Off flew the baseball cap.

Out fell a sheen of chestnut-colored hair.

A solid thud against Cameron's chest almost knocked him off his feet. He stumbled and did a desperate two-step to keep his balance. Groaning in pain, he hoped his good intentions hadn't just rebroken a couple of ribs. His eyes flew open in surprise at the bundle of outrageous womanly curves squirming in his arms. For a moment he was too shocked to do more than gape in disbelief. Never had he seen a prettier pair of big brown eyes than those widening in alarm.

A furious flutter settled itself in his groin as an unforeseen energy passed between them like an electric current. Rooted to the spot as if he were standing up to his knees in water, Cameron felt an overwhelming sexual surge rush through every cell in his body. It was downright unsettling. He hadn't felt this kind of intensity since indulging in his first adolescent fantasies. Recalling the basic tenets of electricity, he wondered whether they would both be blown to smithereens the second he set her down.

Such dubious logic mocked him. Cameron Wade was too well-grounded to be entertaining such fanciful notions as chemical magnetism or, God forbid, love at first sight. A fickle little gold digger by the name of Bonnie had eradicated such hogwash from his mind long ago.

"Sorry for dropping in on you unannounced this way," Cameron managed to stammer, setting his curvaceous package down at last.

A husky, breathless voice wound itself sensuously around every tingling nerve ending in his body. "I'm afraid I'm the one who should be apologizing for *that*. I'm not usually in the habit of falling into men's arms..."

Cornball. Pure cornball.

Pat Erhart could not believe she had just uttered such a lame line. But then again neither could she believe that she had literally fallen into such a phenomenally strong pair of arms. Arms like that, she decided, should be on the cover of a slick magazine hawking the sex secrets of the stars or some other such equally inane subject. Searching the depths of a pair of blue eyes as piercingly clear as a mountain stream, Pat got the distinct impression that this particular hunk wasn't the type who would go in for that sort of thing.

Upon closer inspection, he was slightly short of perfection. There was the hint of gray in his trim mustache. Weathered around the edges, this tall, lanky blonde wore the look of a battle-scarred warrior. He struck her as a man used to working with his hands. A man willing to fight for that which was his.

No, a pretty-boy magazine layout definitely would not appeal to such a man.

And darned if that didn't make him all the more attractive. Not that Pat had any false hopes about this Western Adonis being similarly drawn to her. She knew that the flicker of interest heating up those gorgeous eyes would be duly put out the instant he put two and two together and came up with three small, needy children.

"What can I do for you, Mr.—?"

"Wade," he supplied. "Cameron Wade."

Perplexed by a strange "tom-tom" noise in the background, Cameron was reminded of those old Westerns he had loved as a child. He found himself wondering if a tribe of renegades was preparing to wage war upon some unsuspecting settlers. Pulling the signed copy of his contract from his pocket, he tried inserting a rational note into his voice as he looked around her.

"I'm here to see Pat about the foreman's job."

Glancing at the familiar signature on the bottom of the page, Pat realized this sexy hunk was under the impression that she was a man. Though it wasn't the first time this had happened and probably wouldn't be the last, she nonetheless bristled at his hasty assumption.

If Cameron Wade shared the same sexist beliefs as most of the other men she'd encountered in this frontier bastion, he would soon be telling her in a polite and condescending voice that such a ''purty little lady'' was far too fragile to be running an operation like this all by herself.

No matter that even when he had been around to help, Hadley had left most of the physical labor to her. No matter that she had been running things around here since long before his untimely death. No matter that neither one of them had the slightest background in ranching. When children were involved, at least one parent had to be responsible—and mature enough to dismiss those girlish butterflies tickling her tummy as nothing more than the aftereffects of a near-tragic fall.

She self-consciously removed her heavy work gloves and extended him her hand in the familiar Western custom.

''Pleased to meet you,'' Pat said looking him straight in the eye, only to find herself utterly lost in their blue, blue depths.

She noted the length of time it took a pregnant pause to give birth to a full-fledged embarrassing moment. Had it not been so utterly insulting, she might have found the look of utter consternation upon Cameron Wade's face funny.

Belatedly he took her hand. It was rough and callused, her grip firm and warm. No manicured pair had ever sent such a jolt of pure sexual awareness thrumming through him like these honest hands. He stared at her in disbelief.

''You're Pat?''

''One and the same.''

Fused by the voltage welding his hand to hers, Cam-

eron studied the woman at length. Devoid of all traces
of makeup, she was remarkably striking. Not pretty in
the usual sense of glamor queens, but an oxymoronic
aura of strength and softness emanating about her left
little doubt in his mind that this lady was more woman
than most men could handle.

Had worry put the first signs of wrinkles around those
incredibly soft eyes? He doubted age could be the culprit. She certainly didn't look old enough to be mother
to three children.

Gingerly, Cameron ran a hand over his rib cage. Was
it his heart hammering against his chest like a sledge-
hammer that was sending that sharp pain through his
torso, or had he actually managed to undo all the time
he'd spent in the hospital by playing a Good Samaritan
without giving thought to his own well-being? He was
grateful to discover that, though tender to the touch, his
ribs did not appear to be rebroken.

He shook his head as if trying to figure out just exactly where he had taken the wrong turn on the way to
Wonderland. Despite the deteriorating condition of the
house and the awful name change the new owner had
given the ranch, the familiar landmarks of his youth
were all about him. He found himself wondering what
kind of a screwball name the E.M.U. was anyway. The
acronym sounded more like a college to him than a
respectable cattle ranch. Fortifying himself with the
thought that it wouldn't be long before he rechristened
it the Triple R, he sucked in his breath and focused his
attention on the provisional three-month contract he
held in his hand.

He had been thrilled when it had arrived in response
to his inquiry, just in time for his release from the hospital. Gleefully abandoning his drafty institutional

gown, he left word of his whereabouts with his manager
and left Vegas with but one thought on his mind: to
hasten the inevitable resolution of a lifelong dream.
That of reclaiming the family ranch and restoring the
Wade name to its own proud position.

He shook his head in disgust. Things were even
worse than he had imagined. A faded old gentleman
stripped of his dignity, the house looked shabby at best.
The paint was weathered and peeling. One shutter hung
by a nail. Another was missing altogether. A broken
window stared at him as reproachfully as a black eye,
and the porch where he had spent countless hours playing now looked more suitable for kindling than anything
else.

The only thing not in disrepair that he could discern
from initial observations was the fencing. That in itself
was a puzzle. Who in his right mind would string expensive chain link all the way around a corral?

Finding his voice at last, Cameron asked in a tone
more brusque than intended. "This is the E.M.U.
Ranch, isn't it?"

Though Pat's eyes twinkled with undisguised amusement, the lilt in her voice stopped just short of laughter.
"Surely you understood emu isn't the name of the
ranch...it's what we raise here."

"Excuse me?"

Cameron wheeled around to pinpoint the source of
that strange sound which had him so befuddled. A huge
ostrichlike creature strutted out of the barn to regard
their visitor with curiosity and what Cameron was certain was mutual distrust.

Tom, tom, tom, tom, tom, thrummed the bird territo-
rially.

Cameron glanced back and forth between the bird

and the woman, searching for the hidden technology that would ultimately land him on *Candid Camera*. Was this somebody's idea of a practical joke? It was a good one, he'd grant 'em that. A real knee-slapper. The Triple R a bird farm? It was as believable as him winning that gargantuan National Championship belt buckle for breaking Shetland ponies. Had it not been for the fact that the woman standing next to him gave no indication whatsoever that anything was amiss, he would have laughed out loud.

"You are joking, aren't you?"

Pat merely shook her head at the scowl that defied her to answer truthfully.

"I'll be a son of a—"

It took an act of conscious self-control to bite back the oath scalding the tip of his tongue. Even then, gentlemanly restraint didn't stop him from leaning his full, formidable height of six feet and three inches over her and bellowing, "Just what have you done to *my* ranch, lady? Grandpa'd do back flips in his grave if he knew you'd turned the Triple R into some kind of damned Yuppie petting zoo. Not to mention the field day the press could have with the news that I've signed on to be a bird wrangler."

Pat wondered if she would have to sew the top of this man's head back on. What was he ranting about? The jumble of words was coming so fast and furious that it was hard to make sense of them.

"Hell and damnation, I signed on to work for a real ranch, not some overgrown chicken farm!"

"They're emus," Pat repeated as patiently as if she were explaining it to a two-year-old.

"If you think for even one minute that I'm sticking

around to work with a flock of dodo birds on steroids, you're out of your mind!''

Pat's hands went to her hips. She'd had quite enough of this cowboy's tirade. Why, the way the man was acting, you'd think he had a personal stake in the ranch. Clearly the fellow wasn't quite right in the head, but seeing how he was the only one who had applied for the job, she couldn't afford to let him off the hook just because he was capable of throwing a bigger temper tantrum than any of her children.

"Let me remind you, Mr. Wade," she said speaking slowly and standing on her tippy toes to lessen the intimidating factor of his height, "that whether you like it or not, I am your boss for at least the next three months. And any respectable man would honor that contract.''

"You deceiving, little—" Cameron shook the contract in question right in the woman's startled face. "Maybe I should have let you fall on that thick head of yours to knock some sense into it!"

Pat exhaled with enough force to ruffle the bangs over her forehead. "I didn't deceive anyone. In fact I purposely capitalized all the letters in the word emu so you'd know exactly what you were getting into. It's not my fault you didn't take the time to find out that emu was no more the name of this ranch than Pat is singularly used as a man's name! As we both well know, ignorance is no excuse in the eyes of the law. You signed on, mister, and by God, you're mine from at least now until winter sets in.''

The last time someone had the audacity to talk to Cameron like this, he'd sent the joker through a plate-glass window. He hated the way women used their sex as an excuse to blurt out whatever they felt like saying without regard to consequence. No matter how pretty this one was, he for one wasn't about to be bullied by someone who barely came up to his chin.

"For your information, I don't belong to anyone. And if you don't think so, just watch how fast I walk away from this bird-brained operation of yours!"

The exact opposite of this belligerent cowboy, whose voice paralleled his temper, when Pat was angry, her voice dropped several cool degrees. When she spoke again, her words were cold enough to freeze-dry the blazing Wyoming sun overhead.

"That contract is legally binding, and the only way you're walking away from here is if I fire you."

In fact, nothing could have made Pat happier at the moment than to send this macho cowboy down the road with an imprint of her boot upon his sexy derriere. Unfortunately, she was far too desperate to let pride get in the way of good sense. Circumstances had left her a widow with three small children and a ranch in dire need of repairs. She had tried telling Hadley that making a go of an emu ranch smack-dab in the middle of cattle country wouldn't be the cakewalk he thought it would be. He hadn't listened of course. Once he was off on one of his get-rich-quick schemes, there was as much chance of stopping Hadley Erhart as the guard rail that had given way and left him dead at the bottom of Red Canyon one snowy night.

Cameron's eyes narrowed. "Do you mean to tell me you'd try keeping a man here against his will?"

His words conjured up for Pat all sorts of improper sexual images utilizing ropes and handcuffs. She dismissed the innuendo with a haughty swipe of the hand.

"Nobody forced you to sign that contract."

Lady or no, Cameron was just about to tell this brassy

little firecracker where she could put her legally binding contract, when he felt the barrel of a gun poked into the small of his back.

"Freeze, varmint!"

Two rascals wearing battered cowboy hats, shorts emblazoned with cartoon characters, and worn, dusty boots regarded him from behind matching scowls. Drawn by the commotion, Johnny and Kirk Erhart had been covertly watching the heated interplay as intently as any full-fledged theatrical production. With a trail of improvised cowboy paraphernalia dragging behind them, the two boys rushed to their mother's defense.

"Reach for the sky!"

While one boy kept his plastic gun steady against the interloper's back, the other gathered a loop of rope into his hands. Hoping they weren't contemplating a hanging, Cameron raised his hands in mock surrender.

Clearly he had been ambushed.

"Johnny!" his mother scolded. "How many times have I told you not to point that at anyone?"

"Mom..." the child said in embarrassment before regaining his stage presence. "Keep 'em up there where I can see 'em."

His finger twitching on the trigger of his cap gun, the older boy informed Cameron with genuine Western resolve. "Around these parts, mister, a man stands by his word."

What the woman's ire had not evoked in Cameron, a child's innocence had—a sense of guilt. Johnny, the woman had called him. Darned if the kid didn't remind him some of himself at that age. Cameron fought the urge to run his hand through the lad's shaggy, sandy-colored hair.

An image of another little boy standing in the shadows of the Wind River Mountains came back to him as clearly as if it had been recorded for posterity. Tears streaming down his face, the child had linked hands with his mother and vowed to someday "show 'em all that a Wade could never be beaten." Almost two decades had passed since the seed of that particular promise had been planted. Time enough for Cameron to cultivate a way of returning home an unprecedented success, reclaim the land he considered his birthright, and turn it into one of the finest operations in the country.

There was more than just a little self-indulgent gratification involved in his game plan, and he knew it. Knew it and accepted it as part of why he was the man he was. The kind of man who wouldn't let a couple of broken ribs in the semifinals of the National Rodeo Championship stop him from achieving his dream. The kind of man determined to overcome any obstacles in his path, no matter how large—or how small...

A funny ache settled in the pit of Cameron's stomach as he studied the stubborn set of this little boy's jaw. He wondered how he would have reacted at that age had someone come onto their property and commenced yelling at *his* mother.

"That's all right, ma'am," Cameron said, squatting on his haunches to meet the child at eye level. "I understand that a man's got to do what it takes to protect what's his."

Johnny seemed to visibly grow an inch. Off to the side a couple of paces, his brother holstered his toy gun.

"You're not really gonna break a promise you made to my mom, are you?" The look the boy gave him was so piercing that it almost made Cameron forget why he was here.

Almost.

Gruffly he reminded himself that he wasn't here on a charity case. Having limited interaction with them, he didn't even particularly like kids. His job here was not to rescue anyone, but rather to kick this pushy mommy and her brood off *his* ranch before she tried bamboozling him with those unusually long eyelashes. It suddenly occurred to Cameron that the best way to accomplish his purpose was not by butting heads with her. No matter that she had made a laughingstock of the Triple R, it was after all in his best interest to stick around awhile.

"All right, lady. You win."

Cameron capitulated with a bona fide grin that activated a matching pair of dimples on either side of his mouth. He'd have to remember to thank Johnny later for providing him an opportunity to squeeze out of the corner he'd backed himself into.

"Whether your contract is legally binding or not, it's lucky for you that I'm a man of my word. Looks like you've got yourselves a prisoner, boys."

Wondering exactly what she'd let herself in for, Pat contemplated Cameron's use of the word *lucky*. It was obvious that Johnny and Kirk were fascinated by the rough-and-tumble cowboy who looked like he'd just stepped off the set of their favorite television series. That phony line about him being a man of his word certainly sounded like a load of typical Hollywood hype to her. Pat's cynical thoughts were interrupted by her youngest son's most frequently uttered complaint.

"I'm hungry."

"I just fed you," she responded with a telltale sigh.

"But that was *hours* ago."

It was at that precise moment that the baby decided

she had been ignored long enough. Flinging her bottle
out of the playpen, Amy protested her prolonged captivity with an ear-splitting wail intended to let anyone
within a mile radius know of her unhappiness.

Cameron watched Pat's eyelids drift shut in weariness. "Go get your sister, boys," she instructed, "and
I'll get started on dinner."

It wasn't every day a real live cowboy landed on their
front steps, and certainly not one who appeared willing
to indulge them in a game of make-believe. Conse-
quently, Johnny delegated the mundane chore to his little brother.

"Kirk, you go get Amy while I take the prisoner to
the hoosegow."

Pat graced Cameron with an amused smile. "You can
take that to mean the house. Hopefully you and I will
be able to have a calmer discussion about terms of your
new job over dinner."

Proud of the way she uttered the words as smoothly
as if she were looking at the man's résumé instead of
the hard plane of his chest, she added as an afterthought,
"That'll give me a chance to thank you properly for
saving me from breaking my neck earlier."

Although Cameron could think of a variety of ways
that this fiery little number could show her appreciation,
he doubted whether any of them were what she had in
mind. He tried bridling those wayward thoughts, but his
lazy smile nonetheless made Pat remember for the first
time in a very long while that she was a woman as well
as a mother.

Chapter Two

Hoping to stop the boys' squabble over who was supposed to be in charge of the baby, Cameron paused on his way to the "hoosegow" to emancipate the squalling toddler from her playpen. There was no benevolence in the act; he wanted only to put an end to the tot's deafening howls for attention. It was little wonder her mother was crazy. In his opinion, anyone forced to endure that kind of nerve-grating caterwauling for more than one solid minute just might have a right to be.

To his complete and utter surprise, the baby stopped crying the instant he picked her up. Grateful for small miracles, Cameron mutely bore the fruit-stained kiss she planted upon his cheek as she nestled against his chest with a satisfied coo. Her actions only confirmed his theory that women were genetically programmed from birth to manipulate men. A femme fatale at this tender age would undoubtedly turn a mother prematurely gray and a father bald.

Which, by the way, made him wonder where the heck

the man of the house was, anyway. Cameron was anxious to see what kind of elusive louse expected a
woman to reshingle a house all by herself. He hadn't
noted a ring on Pat's finger, but then again Cameron
wouldn't exactly expect her to wear one while doing
such physically exacting work.

"For crying out loud!" he exclaimed, shaken from
his errant thoughts by a growing wet spot down the
front of his clean, new shirt.

One didn't have to be Dr. Spock to discern the cause
to be a leaky diaper. Loosening the baby's sticky hands
from around his neck, Cameron thrust her from him as
if she were a package of nitroglycerin. As far as he was
concerned, all children should come wrapped in cellophane with detailed warning labels attached.

"Keep on moving, mister," Johnny directed him at
the end of his plastic barrel.

Cameron gritted his teeth as he foisted the baby into
Kirk's thin arms. Not used to being bossed around by
anyone, it was especially galling to bend his will to a
ten-year-old's. As he took his first faltering steps toward
captivity, Cameron could have sworn that big goofy-
looking bird in the corral winked at him.

Pat paused to watch her children interact with her
new foreman. Considering his overtly hostile reaction
to her, he was actually being a pretty darned good
sport—or prisoner, rather—as Johnny directed him at
gunpoint up the back steps. Pushed back at a rakish
angle, Cameron's black felt cowboy hat allowed his hair
to fall carelessly across his forehead. Pat couldn't help
but notice how the dark blond color was shot through
unevenly with streaks of sunshine. Suddenly he looked

far less a broad-shouldered ruffian than a charming
grown up version of her own two little imps.

Albeit an incredibly virile version.

Startled by the womanly reaction that curled her
stomach up in a tight ball and sent handfuls of tingles
racing through her body in a flash of heat, Pat was
amazed that some stranger could waltz into her front
yard, pluck her in midair like a pop fly and simultaneously make her wish she was wearing something soft
and sexy. She thought she had buried those feelings
with her husband, and it terrified her to think of them
resurfacing. As a mother and businesswoman, she had
more than enough to handle with a clear head, let alone
one filled with the stuff and nonsense of romantic fairy
tales.

Once upon a time, Pat had been young and naive
enough to fall for such balderdash—and had spent the
duration of her life paying for it. Ignoring her parents'
repeated warnings that Hadley Erhart's pockets were as
empty as his promises, she had eloped at eighteen,
pledging herself one hundred percent to each of her husband's successive ventures. Unfortunately, Hadley had
a habit of expending more energy in the engineering of
his next get-rich-quick scheme than in the arduous process of making any of them actually work. As his stern
father-in-law commented at his funeral, Hadley was a
whole lot better at starting things than finishing them.

It was less allegiance to her late husband's memory
than a commitment to abandon the gypsy life they had
lived, hopping from one risky endeavor to another that
kept Pat so stubbornly rooted to this place. The moment
she'd laid eyes upon it, she had fallen in love with this
run-down old ranch. It had as much character as the
mountain range just outside her back door. Life in the

shadows of those larger-than-life mountains was hard, no question about it. But, isolated from the problems of more populous areas, the soil in Wyoming was good for growing happy, healthy children.

Even though the local naysayers were laying bets against her chances of surviving just one winter, Pat was determined to make a real home for her family right here. And if that meant having to humble herself by making dinner for some obnoxious cowboy who openly regretted saving her neck, then so be it.

"Make yourself comfortable," she said, clearing off a spot for Cameron on the sofa and casting an embarrassed look at the abandoned toys cluttering the room, "while I get started on dinner."

Short of declaring it a national disaster area, there was nothing she could do about the state of disarray of her house. Fixing supper was the priority of the moment. Simple fare like peanut butter sandwiches or macaroni and cheese generally sufficed for their evening meal, but one look at those long legs stretched across her living room floor sent that idea skittering away like a sunbeam upon rushing water. It was highly unlikely that a man as big as Cameron would be satisfied with her usual laissez-faire attitude toward food.

Pat would have liked to have impressed her new employee with her culinary talents. Unfortunately, the empty pantry was a reflection of her checkbook. She could only hope that her new foreman was handier with a hammer than Hadley had been. The last thing she needed around here was another helpless man with an appetite to match his impressive frame.

As if worried Cameron might attempt an escape, Johnny and Kirk took their places on either side of their prisoner on the couch and settled in for their favorite television program. It was an animated version of an old Western, underscored by the timeless theme of good versus bad. The last time he'd watched a show where the heroes and villains were so easily identified by the color of their hats, he'd been no older than the two boys who held him captive.

Cameron glanced uncomfortably at his own dark hat resting on the edge of the sofa. Like a dog trying to rid itself of a pesky flea, he tried shaking the feeling off. It wasn't as if God had personally assigned him to this family's troubles. He had more than enough of his own to handle. Cameron reminded himself that his primary objective was to ascertain just how cheaply he could buy back the old place. And do so before he became emotionally attached to the "squatters" who were presently attached to it. He knew that anything more would simply be tempting fate.

Out of the corner of his eye, Cameron caught a glimpse of the woman working in the kitchen. He snapped his head around in a double take. It looked like she was attacking an avocado with a hammer. A second look determined that it was in fact the biggest, *greenest* egg he had ever seen. While green eggs and ham might be a suitable meal for Dr. Seuss, the very thought made Cameron's stomach quiver.

Ten minutes later he found himself seated before the world's largest omelet. Milk, home-canned apples, and garden-fresh salad accompanied it. Ever vigilant, Johnny and Kirk flanked him on both sides. Amy sat beside her mother in a high chair that had been mended too often with great gobs of duct tape.

Despite the growling in his stomach, Cameron was about to beg off the main course when a familiar voice echoed through his mind. "People whose manners are

absent probably are missing more than just their manners. No matter how old you get, son, or how important
you might think you've become, just remember your
mother raised you right and act accordingly.''

Rose Wade had been dead for almost fifteen years,
but Cameron felt her presence in this house as surely
as when she had taught him respect at her table. A lump
formed in his throat. As inexplicably as a moth is drawn
to a flame, Cameron's memories had led him back home
in search of that which had been stolen from him. Was
it innocence, he wondered, or pride?

An obedient son, he complied with his mother's
ghostly command. Sectioning off a tiny piece of omelet,
he took a hesitant bite. To his astonishment, it was quite
tasty.

He lifted his gaze from his plate to discover Pat waiting for his reaction. She looked so anxious and so lovely
sitting there that his heart swelled up in his chest like
an overinflated balloon.

"Not bad," he commented, taking another mouthful.

Cameron watched the hardness around her eyes
soften. He was on the verge of encouraging her to use
that dynamite smile of hers a little more often when a
handful of egg drilled him square in the forehead.

"Amy!" her mother cried out in horror.

Undaunted, the tot launched her spoon into space
where it did a double somersault before landing in the
middle of their guest's dinner plate.

The boys roared as Amy clapped her hands in glee.

"I'm so sorry," Pat stammered, coming at Cameron
with a napkin.

"No harm done, ma'am," he said, stopping his red-
faced hostess in her tracks with a careless wave of the

hand. "It isn't the first time I've had egg on my face, and I doubt it'll be the last."

Pat was impressed by this gruff cowboy's tact. She knew few men who would have handled the incident half as graciously. The instant the poor man had stepped onto her property, he'd been beset by calamity—from women dropping from the sky into his arms, being captured by the infamous Erhart Boys, to being ambushed at the dinner table. Watching him wipe the splatters from his once clean Western-cut shirt, she could hardly blame Cameron for his lack of enthusiasm about signing on at Fort Bedlam.

Inwardly railing against the formal "ma'am" which made her feel like her own world-weary mother, she suggested, "Why don't you just call me Pat? Everybody does."

A candid appraisal glittered in Cameron's eyes. "If you don't mind my saying, Patricia suits a pretty woman better."

The blood in her veins began to bubble under the heat of the glance that took her in head to toe. A hot blush crept up her neck. It was silly how pleased she was by the offhanded compliment.

Lordy, had she completely forgotten what it was like to have a man flirt with her? Having done both a man and a woman's job for so very long, she had almost come to think of herself in androgynous terms. The gentle reminder that she had another name besides Mom made her suddenly feel as giddy as a teenager.

Smoothing a wisp of stray hair back from her face, she tossed him a disarming smile. "Patricia's just fine with me. Now if you have any questions about the job, this would be a good time to ask them."

Unfortunately the question uppermost in Cameron's mind was not one he thought should be asked in front of children. Over the years on the rodeo circuit, he'd had more than his fair share of made-up, coifed tarts bat their mascaraed eyelashes at him. Why none of them made him feel as overtly sexual, as purely animalistic as his new boss did with a simple smile was beyond him. He wondered exactly what it was about this unpretentious woman masquerading as a teenager in those baggy overalls that was so unbelievably sexy it set his heart ticking like an overwound five-dollar watch.

"Just one," he said, giving voice to the question that he had been wanting to ask ever since this woman had tumbled from the roof into his arms like some fallen angel.

"Where's your husband?" *And doesn't he know he's a fool to leave you here all alone?*

Patricia glanced quickly at the children. She was not yet comfortable discussing their father's death in front of them. It was a wound still too raw to the touch. Though far from being a good provider by society's standards, Hadley had seldom raised his voice let alone a hand to his children. They missed him terribly.

"I'm a widow," she said softly.

Cameron's fork clattered against his plate. His eyes looked everywhere in the room but at her.

His embarrassment was almost audible. Patricia hadn't meant to make him squirm. After all, he had no part in the cruel hand fate had dealt her. She asked the boys to get more milk from the refrigerator and, once they were out of earshot, plunged into an abbreviated version of Hadley's death with the swiftness of a surgeon working without anesthesia.

"A little less than a year ago my husband was killed in a car wreck. The roads were icy, he'd been drinking and the guardrail didn't hold. The coroner assured me his death was instantaneous."

A lump lodged itself sideways in Cameron's throat. He couldn't imagine a single mother attempting to run this ranch all by herself while raising three tiny human tornadoes. The only sound he could hear in the deafening silence that followed her account was that of his own heartbeat.

"I'm sorry," he said simply.

It was inadequate, but he could think of nothing else to add as the boys slid back into their seats beside him. When he had impetuously signed that contract back in the hospital, it hadn't occurred to him that he might actually come to give a tinker's damn about the people he intended running off this place. He had expected to be greeted by some rich, hobbyist rancher. Not a vulnerable, young widow with spunk enough to put a chink in his well-polished emotional armor.

Cameron didn't fancy himself a sentimental man, but he figured he'd have to be blind not to notice how bare the cupboards were, how thin the children were, how desperate the woman was. He would have had to have been made of granite not to want to kiss away the furrows worrying her lovely brow. To sample the sweetness of those full, inviting lips…

Criminey! He had no more control of his thoughts than of a wild mustang roaming the range. Good sense warned him to get out while the getting was good. The very thought of working on a bird ranch was an insult to his dignity. No self-respecting cowboy would be caught dead *eating* one of these overgrown chickens let alone acting as foreman for what was certain to be the

most unpopular ranch in the county. The jeers and jibes
were already ringing in his ears. Some of the announc-
ers on the circuit had taken to introducing him as the
Big Man. Cameron wasn't particularly eager to trade in
that moniker for the Bird Man.

"So can I count on you staying the next three
months?" Patricia asked, naming the time frame out-
lined in the contract she'd drawn up.

Cameron twisted uncomfortably in his seat. Darned
if the whole family wasn't looking at him like he was
Saint Michael himself sent to rescue them from Satan's
clutches. He hoped that Patricia had registered her children's big ol' pleading eyes as lethal weapons down at
the local police station. He hadn't felt this much pressure in the arena with thousands of eyes trained on his
performance.

"Pleeeeeease stay," Kirk begged.

"On the cowboy trail, a promise made is a promise
kept," Johnny interjected with all the solemnity of an
old-time hanging judge.

Cameron signaled capitulation with a heavy sigh.

"Three months and not a day longer," he grumbled.
"And there are a couple of things we need to set
straight right from the get-go."

Raising her eyebrows, Patricia waited patiently for
him to continue.

"You can count on me to do the dirtiest, hardest
work you need done—without complaint. Fencing, roofing, painting. It doesn't much matter to me. I've even
been known to fix a broken-down motor or two, but I'm
telling you right up front, I'm no bird wrangler."

A smile played on Patricia's lips. "You wouldn't
happen to be afraid of them, would you?"

At the affront, Cameron puffed up like a blowfish.

Each word was a single, crisp word as it came from his mouth. "No, I wouldn't."

Johnny irreverently tucked his hands beneath his armpits and flapped his elbows in comic relief. Kirk joined in.

"Cluck, cluck, cluck..."

Cameron glared threateningly from one to the other. A menacing sneer twitched beneath his mustache, and the last cluck died a tortured death.

"Boys, I'm sure Mr. Wade is no chicken," Patricia chided gently before turning her attention upon the bird in question. "And you can rest assured that the children and I are more than capable of tending to the emus ourselves. If you would just be so kind as to take care of some of the major repairs around here, you will more than meet your contractual obligations."

The fire illuminating those chocolate-colored eyes of hers led Cameron to believe that the lady was definitely a survivor. Having spent years being pursued by a bevy of buckle bunnies, he'd all but forgotten that there might actually be honest women left in the world. Those prolific bunnies earned their name by chasing after the trophy buckles worn by big-name rodeo winners on the circuit. Cameron knew it was more than their prize money these women sought. There was also vicarious prestige in associating with a champion. After being worked over by their veritable queen two summers ago, Cameron had become impervious to their charms. He had, in fact, become so disillusioned with all women after Bonnie had shown him the indisputable facts of life that his number-one rule for dating thereafter had been to use them before they could use him.

"I'll tackle your roof first thing in the morning," he said, pushing his chair away from the table. "Now, why don't we discuss the particulars of our living arrangements while I give you a hand with the dishes?''

Because I can't afford to break every dish in the house! Patricia thought to herself in a sudden rush of panic. The mere thought of telling this virile cowboy where to bed down made her quiver like a jackrabbit lippety-lopping across the rifle range on the opening day of hunting season. Unfortunately, her protests that he didn't need to help with the dishes were to no avail. Though patently old-fashioned enough to believe that the most physically demanding tasks on a ranch belonged solely to the male of the species, Cameron had been well schooled early on by his mother that there simply was no such thing as ''women's work.''

Chapter Three

Patricia became even more flustered when Cameron rolled up his sleeves to reveal a pair of strong, muscled forearms. Wielding a clean dishcloth with the potency of a ninja warrior, the man somehow managed to look as sexy in the kitchen as she imagined he would in the bedroom. Remembering how safe and secure she had felt earlier in the day, wrapped in the embrace of those masculine arms, was almost enough to make her drop the plate she was holding. Up to her elbows in soapy water, Patricia tried washing away the disturbing feelings that close proximity with this man evoked in her.

Since Hadley had been even less help in the kitchen than he had been outdoors, she was unaccustomed to having a man underfoot in her strictly feminine domain. Cameron, on the other hand, seemed completely at ease in his surroundings, rummaging through drawers and putting things away with minimal fuss. Before being excused to do their homework, the boys helped clear the table, and though the expediency of completing this mundane daily chore broke all previous records, Patricia couldn't quite bring herself to feel grateful for Cameron's assistance. Not when simply brushing against his thigh while handing him a cleanly rinsed glass sent a wave of electrical current dancing across her skin.

It was crazy. Never had a man had such a completely befuddling effect upon her. If an accidental touch could make her feel this way, she wondered what effect his kisses might have. The guilt of such a thought weighing heavy on her mind, Patricia attacked the dirty dishes with all the determination of a gladiator.

"You're going to rub the pattern right off that plate," Cameron commented with a knowing smile.

The water in the sink was growing hotter by the minute. Patricia knew it had less to do with the temperature of the water flowing out of the tap than with the traitorous hormones turning the blood in her veins to molten lava. Perturbed that Cameron was so obviously aware of her discomfort, she hoped some light conversation would help lessen the tension lodged squarely at the base of her neck.

"Did you say that your grandfather was somehow connected with this place?" she ventured.

Cameron harrumphed so loudly that it made Patricia jump.

"Connected to it, hell! He *owned* it."

Anger ignited his eyes with blue fire as he continued. "Showed up here one day on a stallion he called Midnight with nothing more than a Colt .45 strapped to his hip. Staked out a claim as far as the eye could see and said 'This is mine.'"

Unable to understand why her question had upset him so, Patricia expressed her dismay. "Without compunction to how the Native Americans who were here first might have felt about that?''

Cameron merely guffawed at the naïveté of her inquiry. ''Spencer Wade wasn't the kind of man to take such things into consideration. By all accounts he was a tough, old bird, weathering freezing winters and hostile renegades with the same unflinching resolve. There was a good reason he kept that .45 well oiled and within reach. Any sleazy snake-oil-selling banker ever had the gall to try holding him hostage with a little piece of paper would have met with a blaze of gunfire.''

The pride was unmistakable in Cameron's voice. The silence that followed this cryptic outburst was as heavy as a fog bank. Patricia drove through it blind.

''Is *that* why you answered my ad? Are you on some kind of nostalgia trip?''

''Something like that,'' he retorted with a strange look in his eye.

''I take it then that Grandpa didn't exactly want to sell the ranch?''

''The Wades never sold out. This land was stolen from us plain and simple.''

The sponge that Patricia was holding fell into the sudsy water with a plop. Had she heard him right?

''Stolen?''

''Legalized theft.''

The words came out of Cameron's mouth like bullets. Hard and fast. ''About twenty years ago the economy around here took a dive. The president called it a recession at the time, but things weren't nearly as bad as the banks wanted folks to believe. They took advantage of the situation to call in the loans on several ranches. The Triple R was one of them.''

He didn't have the heart to expound further. The

memory of his father, a kind and gentle man by nature, broken by the greed of a few unscrupulous opportunists could bear no more contemplation than the last two decades had already born. The thought of his father now confined to a cubicle in a retirement home brought a familiar tightness to his chest. Personally he thought the Eskimos' tradition of setting their old people adrift on icebergs was preferable to the sterile, drawn-out death his father had so selflessly chosen for himself. The last time Cameron had visited him, he had apologized repeatedly for letting "the old man" and his own boys down.

Even from the grave, Spencer Wade threw a long shadow over his only son who, despite a lifetime of trying, had never been able to live up to his legendary expectations. Cameron was torn between love of his father and pride of the gruff grandfather who had taught him how to ride his first horse. Just as soon as the Triple R was back in his hands, he vowed to bring his father back home and lay away the ghosts of the past.

Once and for all.

Patricia felt a tiny shudder of foreboding at the determined look on Cameron's face. "Do you fancy yourself a little like your grandfather?" she asked hesitantly.

The question was astute enough to coax a lopsided smile from him. "Well, I'd wager we'd both feel the same way about turning this ranch into a foul playpen for the ugliest flock of chickens I've ever seen."

A smile danced in Patricia's eyes. "Fowl play did you say?"

Cameron groaned at the tortured pun. Patricia giggled. And just as quickly as the sun bursts though the clouds on an overcast day, melancholy reminiscences turned to light, easy banter.

As Patricia went about the business of getting two seemingly inexhaustible little boys tucked into their respective beds, Cameron sank into a worn, comfortable recliner and closed his eyes—for all of ten seconds before Amy Leigh's sudden and shrill cry brought him upright in his chair. He was tempted to call upstairs for Patricia to "do something" with the child but knew how unnecessary that would be. Had she been in the farthest corner of the attic, Patricia would have been able to hear her baby wailing.

Cameron had told his new boss in no uncertain terms that he was no bird wrangler. He thought it went without saying that he was not a baby-sitter. Figuring that if he ignored her bid for attention those little lungs would surely give out sooner or later, he leaned back and closed his eyes again. This particular strategy served only to incense the child, and the volume of her cries increased several decibels. His nerves crackling with the force of her renewed intensity, Cameron felt his blood pressure rise. He pulled a cherished watch fob out of his pocket and checked the time.

Swallowing the curse scalding the tip of his tongue, he hoisted himself out of the comfort of the sagging recliner and made his way over to the mechanical swing into which the child was securely strapped. According to Patricia, this was the best way of putting Amy Leigh to sleep.

He'd hate to see how her other methods worked.

"Stop it," Cameron said firmly in the same tone of voice that had proven effective in training any number of dogs over the years. "Stop it right this instant!"

Eyelashes glistening with tears, Amy stopped only long enough to hold out her pudgy arms to him.

Upstairs, Patricia listened to the boys' nighttime prayers with only one ear. The other one was attuned to Amy's usual prebedtime petulance. Cameron didn't exactly strike her as the patient type with children, so when Amy's cries stopped in the middle of the boys' "God-blesses" just as abruptly as they had begun, she grew worried. Would she come downstairs to find her youngest gagged and trussed up like some unlucky steer?

What Patricia actually found upon her return to the living room was enough to make her shake her head in disbelief. Cameron was dozing in the big chair while her daughter sat in the middle of the floor teething on what appeared to be a genuine solid gold pocket watch.

"Just who is putting whom to sleep?" she asked, coming down the last three creaky steps.

Cameron opened his eyes to regard her with a lazy, insolent gaze. He hadn't been anywhere near asleep but didn't dare say so for fear Patricia would have him running a day care for every toddler in the area tomorrow. Likely she'd claim it was written somewhere in small print in that fool contract he'd signed.

Besides, it had been his experience that women interpreted any attention toward their kids as an open invitation for them to start calling him Daddy. He shuddered at the thought.

The sentimentality that simply being back in this house evoked in him was disturbing to say the least. Why, he'd almost been tempted to pick the little dickens up and rock her to sleep! Cameron blamed this momentary lapse of sanity on the fact that he'd overheard his own name included in the prayers which had floated down the stairs like sweet perfume.

"God bless Cameron."

"And make him stay…"

What a rotten trick, he thought to himself. Cameron wondered if they would still pray for him if they knew he'd come here with the express intention of buying their home out from under them.

Gathering her daughter into her arms, Patricia attempted to take the girl's latest "toy" away from her. The toddler wailed and swatted at her mother's hands, but the deft substitution of a more traditional teething ring quickly pacified her.

Patricia held the watch out to Cameron by its golden chain. It was covered in drool. Wiping it on the hem of her apron, she took the opportunity to study it more closely. Elaborately scrolled into the back were the initials S.W. and below them a date—1909.

"Your grandfather's?" she asked, handing it over with due reverence. Amazingly it was still ticking. She had to bite her tongue to keep from asking if he was crazy. Would anyone but a man let a baby play with such a valuable keepsake?

Cameron nodded, noting that the antique was none the worse for wear. He figured if it could pull through gunfights and prairie fires, the old timepiece should be able to survive a teething little girl. Before putting it back in his pocket, he wound it once for good measure.

"If you'll wait here, I'll put Amy down for the night and be right back."

The intimacy of Patricia's promise wrapped itself around Cameron like sweet cotton candy. That voice of hers was pure magic.

Black magic, he'd wager.

* * *

Whatever magic this stranger had worked on her little fusspot, Patricia was grateful. When Amy was born, the nurses in the maternity ward had pronounced her colicky. As time passed and the baby refused to outgrow her demanding disposition, Patricia resigned herself to the fact that her daughter was simply going to be difficult to raise. Boys, she had heard, would wring a mother's heart through the years. Girls, they said, would rip it out.

She pulled a blanket over Amy and kissed her softly on the cheek. Patricia couldn't help thinking how different their evening routine had been just because of Cameron's presence. How obvious it was that the boys needed a male role model in their lives. How nervous she was around his overt brand of sexuality....

Like a predatory cat feigning indifference, Cameron was waiting for her when she returned to the living room a moment later.

"Looks like you got everybody tucked in but me."

The comment made the blood sing through Patricia's veins.

As if unaware of the twin roses blooming on her cheeks, Cameron continued, "Just where do you want me to sleep?"

In my bed! was the unbidden thought that flashed through Patricia's mind. As a steamy image of this man's naked body stretched leisurely across her bed caused her to trip over her own tongue, an inner voice of reason yelled at her to get a grip. The last time she'd succumbed to such feminine weakness, she'd wound up a mother to three. Four, she silently amended, if you counted Hadley.

Patricia realized with a start that Cameron was looking at her strangely. It wasn't as if he were leering at her; he was simply waiting for an answer to his question. The breath was locked in her lungs. *Speak up!* she ordered her brain.

"In the bunkhouse," she managed at last to sputter. "You'll have to sleep there. It isn't much. Just an old cabin actually..."

Her apology trailed off. There was absolutely no reason that Cameron couldn't stay in the more comfortable main house with them—other than the fact that people were sure to talk, and Patricia wasn't about to subject her children to this small town's rumor mill. The rest of America might be as fashionably liberal as television programming portrayed it, but Lander, Wyoming was still as staunchly conservative as Mayberry, U.S.A. Why, whispered gossip alone had been cause enough for more than one local official to lose his position.

If there was some other reason why Patricia was uncomfortable having Cameron sleeping under the same roof with her, she wasn't ready to analyze it yet.

Little did she know that there was no need to explain about the Spartan living conditions of the bunkhouse. Cameron was familiar with every inch of the place. It had been his grandparents' original homestead, and he had spent many happy childhood days playing in and around the old cabin. He neither expected nor wanted anything as fancy as a telephone or television set, but he did hope it had been updated with modern plumbing.

Ten minutes later Patricia was cutting a narrow swath through the darkness with a flashlight. Carefully, she and Cameron picked their way along the overgrown path connecting the main house to the outbuilding. Once when Patricia stumbled, he reached out to steady her. It had quite the opposite effect.

Spinning, spinning, spinning out of control...Patricia

felt like Alice in Wonderland as she fell against a sky
sprinkled with diamonds, toppled into a whorl of emotions which she was trying desperately to suppress. And
failed.

"Are you all right?" Cameron asked. Warm and soft
in the darkness, his voice was black velvet to the ears.

"Yes," she lied, shining the thin beam of light upon
the bunkhouse door.

As it was never locked, Patricia grasped the knob and
pushed the door open. She fumbled in the blackness for
the string which activated the antiquated light bulb
hanging from the ceiling. It was like searching for a
single dangling spider's thread. When at last it brushed
her knuckles, she grabbed hold and gave a hard tug.
Bathed in the harsh glow of the bare bulb, the cabin's
charm seemed questionable at best.

"Like I said, it isn't much, but it's clean."

"It'll be just fine," Cameron assured her with a smile
so genuine that it measurably reduced the guilt Patricia
was feeling.

Cameron's modest accommodations consisted of an
old brass bed, a couple of high-backed chairs, a braided
rag rug, a small table and a narrow bureau. A sink and
toilet were sectioned off from the rest of the room by a
tiny floral print sheet turned curtain by some handy
seamstress.

"I'll help you make the bed," she said, walking over
to the bureau where the sheets and blankets were kept.

"There's no need," he assured her. "I'm more than
capable of taking care of myself, Patricia."

Something about the way her name rolled off his
tongue as mellifluous as a poem made her go quite soft
inside. How often had she uttered those same self-
assured platitudes about being able to fend for herself?

So many times that her mother claimed she sounded like a broken record. Her father repeatedly assured her that she was wrong in her foolish assumptions. In that smug way of his, Roland D'Winter liked reminding her just how much she relied on him for the benevolence of a roof over her head and clothes on her back. From a young age, Patricia discerned that he would like nothing more than to keep his daughter pinned permanently under his control like one of the more exotic butterflies in his ghastly collection.

"I'm sure you are," she agreed while crisply unfurling a clean white sheet over his bed like a gigantic surrender flag.

Patricia was keenly aware that this was the first time she had been alone with any man in his bedroom other than her husband. Not that this was any swinging bachelor pad or that she flattered herself with any thought that Cameron was interested in her that way. It was just those crazy electrical signals that her body was giving off, warning her of an impending overload.

Cameron tucked an edge of the sheet between the mattress and the frame as Patricia pulled her side taut. It was funny how such an everyday task could become so charged with sexual energy when shared with a good-looking hunk of a cowboy.

Like graceful doves, Patricia's work-worn hands darted across his bedding smoothing out the wrinkles. Cameron couldn't help but wonder why she wasn't wearing her wedding ring. His own father, widowed for many years now, never took his off. Like his beloved Rose, John Wade would be buried with that thin gold band on his finger. Cameron knew he had no right to be judgmental, but he was nonetheless bothered by the symbolic rejection of the wedding vows this woman had taken before God and man. Perhaps Patricia was more like the buckle bunnies of his past than he would like to believe. Was she openly declaring herself available to the next likely prospect willing to take on the financial and emotional burdens of a ready-made family?

As Cameron reached across the bed to even out his covers, he inadvertently brushed fingertips with Patricia. Static electricity arched across the cotton fabric, shocking them both at the same time. Cameron looked across the narrow expanse of the bed into her eyes. They were wide open and shining with distrust and— Was that passion he glimpsed swirling in the depths of those bewitching mahogany-colored orbs? He forced air into his lungs in short, desperate sips.

"Why don't you wear your wedding ring?"

Having already assured himself that this was absolutely none of his business, Cameron wasn't quite sure where the question had come from.

Patricia pulled her hand away from his as if she had been stung and gave it an apologetic look.

"I had to pawn it years ago."

Cameron had expected any response but that one. His mother had once said that the pawning of a wedding ring was the ultimate poverty, the supreme humiliation for a woman. He remembered his parents being poor. He remembered not having as nice things as many of his classmates. He remembered all too vividly the humiliation of losing their ranch. But never once in Cameron's memory could he ever recall his parents so much as discussing the possibility of such desperate measures as selling their wedding rings.

He grabbed a pillow and jammed it into its case with unnecessary roughness. Something about this woman with her proud chin and soft brown eyes elicited in him a protective, tender sentiment that quite frankly scared him to death. Just watching her take a tired swipe at the stray wisp of hair that fell across her cheek made him want to sweep her up in his arms and lay her upon this bed like a bouquet of exotic blossoms. To make passionate, exquisite love to her...

She was talking to him, he realized with a start. Reluctantly Cameron forced his thoughts away from the bed to what it was she was saying.

"You'll take your meals with us, of course, and..." *Why for gosh sakes was it so hard to say it?* "You'll have to use the bathing facilities at the main house. Do you prefer morning or evening showers?"

Patricia hated asking such personal questions, but with a family of four already utilizing the only bathroom in the house, it was imperative that some kind of schedule be formulated as soon as possible. She shuddered at the image of one of the boys pounding on the bathroom door while Cameron was in the shower. She shivered at the thought of herself accidentally walking in on him wearing nothing more than a towel.

"Mornings, if that's all right with you," he replied.

"Mornings it will be then."

They smiled stiffly at each other. Just a couple of hours ago they had been going at one another with their gloves off. Now they stood on opposite sides of a brass bed contemplating the fact that whether either one of them liked it or not, there was clearly as much attraction crackling between them as animosity. What was that old adage about love and hate being separated by a very thin line? This was going to be a far more dangerous arrangement than either one had initially imagined.

If she could have fired him, Patricia would have.

If he could have walked away, Cameron would have.

Speaking volumes with their eyes, they gauged one another warily.

"I should be going," Patricia said at length, pulling a tight smile across her teeth. "If there's anything else you need, please don't hesitate to ask."

Cameron's aroused libido told him that there certainly was something else, but he didn't think goodnight kisses were listed among the benefits in that blasted contract he'd been so eager to sign.

"Everything's fine," he assured her over a heartbeat that mocked him in double time. *Liar, Liar, Liar!* it sang out.

As he held the door open for Patricia to leave, Cameron felt a cold breeze enter the room. It wasn't until she closed it behind her with an echoing "Good night and sleep well," that he realized how her presence had taken the chill from the air.

Sitting on the edge of the newly made bed, he proceeded to take off his boots and make plans for tomorrow. Having come straight from the hospital, he hadn't brought much with him. First thing in the morning he was heading into town to buy a few things from the store.

Cameron lay back into his pillow, closed his eyes and tried to dismiss whatever it was that kept pricking his conscience like a mosquito relentless in its pursuit of blood. Uncomfortable with guilt as a business partner, he reminded himself once again that this opportunity to make his long-cherished dream a reality was no chance happening. Not by a long shot. This was a matter of fate, plain and simple. A matter of destiny. Of universal justice.

Remembering how his father used to refer to the bunkhouse as the doghouse after being banished there once following a rare quarrel with his wife, Cameron wondered how the old man would feel about his dubbing it the birdhouse. Like his father before him, John Wade was a cattle rancher, tried and true. Both of them would have been dismayed by the eerie sounds of piglike grunts and tom-toms which filled the night air. Who would have guessed that emus were so darned loud?

And phew!

As a gentle breeze stirred the air, Cameron discovered his sleeping quarters were downwind of those damnable birds.

Chapter Four

The woman staring back at Patricia from her bathroom mirror the following morning looked far too weary to be only twenty-eight. She sighed. Taking an assessment of one's self at 5:30 in the morning was not a particularly flattering way to start the day. When had the worries weighing down her thoughts imprinted themselves in the fine lines around those once bright eyes? When, for that matter, was the last time she had treated herself to a trip to the beauty shop? Her once stylish cut was now confined to a shaggy ponytail. More often than not it was simply stuffed beneath a baseball cap.

Patricia did not pause to consider why it was on this particular morning that she decided to devote precious minutes to primping. Dabbing a hint of pink peppermint frost on her lips, she assured herself that the only reason she had set the alarm a half an hour earlier than usual was simply to alleviate an inevitable traffic jam outside the bathroom when her newly hired foreman arrived to take his shower. It certainly had nothing to do with pure

feminine interest in a man who had breezed into her life
with the temerity of a tornado.

Nothing whatsoever, she muttered to herself, digging
a dusty curling iron out from under the sink.

There was no question in her mind that the blame for
her restless night's sleep rested squarely on Cameron
Wade's broad shoulders. All night long he had shame-
lessly sauntered in and out of her dreams with his All-
American blond good looks, overt masculinity and mer-
curial disposition, leaving her anxious about his
impending presence at her table—and in her shower.
Not at the same time she was using it, Patricia quickly
amended, but it was too late to prevent her imagination
from running wild with the image of wet, slick skin,
rippling muscles, predatory eyes, and... Residual heat
from the shower coupled with the thought of full-body
exposure and left a sheen of steam upon her bathroom
mirror.

Taking a swipe at her reflection with a washcloth,
she sternly chided herself. "My dear, you are way too
old for such foolishness."

And with that admonition she shelved both her curling iron and her runaway thoughts. After yesterday's
ill-fated introductions, Patricia was determined to make
a better second impression upon Cameron Wade. She
had considerably more faith in her culinary ability than
in the hasty attempt she had made at sprucing herself
up. Undoubtedly it was too much to ask that sizzling
sausage, pancakes and homemade chokecherry syrup
could actually make her new employee glad she had
coerced him into staying. But it sure couldn't hurt any
and would be a nice change from the cold cereal her
family usually shoveled into themselves for breakfast.

* * *

As the cuckoo clock in the living room announced the hour with seven cheerful chirps, the song that Patricia had been humming died on her lips. Time had gotten away from her. She glanced anxiously out the window. Cameron's pickup was gone. Her heart sank at the realization that he'd lit out like some thief in the night.

Patricia's disposition turned as cold as the expensive food she had worked so hard to prepare. As cold as the empty chambers of a woman's injured pride.

Telling herself that a meal and a room for the night would be the cheapest lesson in human nature that she would ever come by, she steeled herself against the children's reaction to the news that their guest had run off.

"Pancakes!" Johnny's eyes opened in surprise at the breakfast in front of him. He took a huge syrup-saturated bite. "Where's Cameron?" he asked, wiping his chin with his pajama sleeve.

"Gone."

The single word stuck in her throat. Patricia took no satisfaction in the knowledge that her suspicions that all men were born liars had once again been proven true. Since her own husband had spent more time running from his problems than facing them, she told herself she shouldn't have expected more from a stranger with no emotional attachments to her plight. Refusing to give in to the temptation to check out the back window one more time, Patricia told herself that there was as much hope of Cameron reappearing as there was of her pulling a rabbit out of a hat; of the bank suddenly waiving the loan on this place; of a frog turning into a prince. Clearly Cameron Wade had sized up her financial status over dinner and convinced himself that she was in no position to legally pursue him for breach of contract.

She wished she could prove him wrong.

"But he promised to show Kirk and me some rope tricks after school today," Johnny protested.

Taking in the disappointed expression on his face, Patricia seethed against all the broken promises in her son's world.

"I'm sorry, honey."

"What'd you do to him?" Johnny glared at his mother as if she were somehow single-handedly responsible for running him off.

"Nothing," Patricia snapped. Certainly nothing she could think of that would send a man fleeing in the wee hours of the morning as if he were afraid of catching some contagious, life-threatening disease.

Kirk stumbled into the room with his shirt half-buttoned.

"Pancakes?" he asked with genuine surprise.

Patricia bristled. As if she *never* fixed them a hot breakfast!

Dragging a pajama sleeve across the bottom of his nose, Johnny informed his younger brother that the newest member of their gang had made a fleet-footed getaway without so much as saying goodbye. Staring disconsolately at the mound of soggy pancakes on the plate his mother thrust before him, Kirk's lower lip quivered.

"I'm sure it's all for the best," Patricia reassured them both with a brittle smile that came nowhere near her eyes. "Now hurry up or you'll be late for school."

All the way down the bumpy road to the bus stop she berated herself for falling for that glib line about Cameron being a man of his word. Certainly the boys were entitled to their despondency, but having no claim to their childish naïveté, she considered her own gull-

ibility a shameful thing. Experience had taught her
men's allegiances were as fleeting as Hadley's dreams.
That a pair of flashing blue eyes was capable of making
her forget that truth was a tribute only to her weakness
as a woman too long without the company of a man.

She returned home a half an hour later resolute in her
determination not to moon around about something over
which she had no control. In no time at all, Patricia was
back in Hadley's old overalls facing a ladder that was
as shaky as her nerves. Yesterday's tumble from the sky
into Cameron's arms hadn't done anything to reduce the
fear of heights that had plagued her since childhood.

Unfortunately, she had little choice but to conquer
her fears. The roof needed fixing, and no one else was
going to volunteer for the job. It was time to put
thoughts of another romantic rescue out of mind.

Don't look down! she cautioned herself with each
step she took. *Whatever you do, don't look down!*

Feeling rather like Charlie Chaplin cast in the role of
a laughable tightrope walker, Patricia made her way
across the sharply peaked roof with the unlikely balance
of a crowbar in her hands. Blood was pounding in her
head, and she fought to breathe deeply so as not to grow
faint. Confined again to a playpen in full sight of her
mother's watchful eye, Amy was too engrossed in the
litter of kittens incarcerated with her to pay much attention to the litany of choice names Patricia called
Cameron in his absence.

Hold on to your heart, Cowboy!

Seeing Patricia up on the roof again twisted Cameron's guts into a couple of half hitches that even the
most seasoned Eagle Scout would be at a loss to undo.
What in God's good name did that woman think she

was doing back up there, when he had specifically told her he was going to fix it himself? Damn her stubborn hide! What was she trying to do? Kill herself?

He stuck his head out the window and hollered before his pickup rolled to a complete stop. ''Get down from there right now before I climb up there myself and drag your pretty little butt down!''

Boiling mad, he wasn't particularly worried about phrasing his concern in politically correct terms. Maybe later when Patricia was safely on the ground and his heart was beating at a normal rate once again, he'd concern himself with matters of semantic sensitivity.

Or maybe he'd use the opportunity to point out that her children minded far better than she did!

''Your mommy is as stubborn as an unbroken colt,'' he muttered as he ran past Amy. In response she dropped a hapless kitten over the side of her playpen directly in his path. The calico scrambled to avoid his size eleven cowboy boots.

Cameron had one foot on the bottom rung of the ladder when Patricia's voice leaked over the edge of the roof. ''You needn't bother making good any quaint he-man threat. I was just about to come down anyway to check on Amy.''

The arctic glare which accompanied that regally intoned announcement would have frozen lesser men on the spot. She looked like she wanted to wrap that crowbar around his neck.

Women!

What confounding creatures they were. What man could ever hope to figure them out? Cameron's aversion for the opposite sex quickly changed to appreciation as Patricia began her descent down that rickety old ladder. Slowly, slowly, slowly...she made her way down step by cautious step. The view from below was quite enjoyable. What that woman could do to a pair of baggy overalls was phenomenal. As that lovely backside moved eye level to him, Cameron cursed his own weakness.

Women!

"Watch out for that broken rung," he instructed, bracing himself against the hope that she just might fall into his arms again.

Patricia snorted at the unnecessary advice.

"That's it." Sensing the nervousness in her rigidity, Cameron spoke as gently as if he were coaxing a skittish filly into a halter. "It's okay. I've got you now."

Things certainly were not okay with Patricia. As his hands encircled her waist, she felt the world tilt crazily off its axis. He set her upon the ground as gently as one would position a butterfly upon a dewy blossom. Railing against the urge to succumb to the security of a pair of arms as strong as forever, she cursed her traitorous body.

Forever! She doubted whether the word was in the scoundrel's vocabulary. In less than twenty-four hours, Cameron Wade had proven he was not the kind of man to be relied upon.

Patricia swatted angrily at his hands.

That *where have you been?* look leveled at him would have brought any sensible husband to his knees but only served to confuse Cameron. Unlike his married friends, he wasn't the type to apologize when he didn't have a clue as to what he'd done wrong.

"What?" he asked throwing his hands up in dismay. This crazy woman's mood had more swings than a confounded playground!

Patricia regarded him through narrowed lids.

"Around here, mister, we start our days when the sun comes up. I'm not paying you to lollygag around till," she pointedly checked her watch, "ten o'clock in the morning."

Instantly defensive, Cameron reminded himself that this was exactly the reason he had pledged wholeheartedly to bachelorhood. Who needed all those demented mind-games women loved to play? Their need to be in control at all times? Their hormonal roller-coaster approach to life in general?

He, for one, was going to be damned hard to break to the double harness. By its very nature, marriage was intended for tamer temperaments than his.

When Cameron spoke again, his words were measured slowly. "I sure as hell don't owe you an explanation of my whereabouts, lady, but for your information I went into town to buy a few things for myself and..." He pointed to his vehicle parked in the driveway. "And for you."

Patricia's anger dissipated at the sight of sunshine glinting off a new aluminum ladder sticking out of the open tailgate of his pickup. Leaden footed, she dragged herself over to peer into the bed of the pickup. Beside stacks of new shingles sat a dozen sacks of groceries. A package of thick T-bones poked out of the top of one.

"You didn't need to do that," she protested, her voice growing small. "You *shouldn't* have done that," she clarified wondering how in the world she was going to pay for all of this.

"Don't think of it as charity," Cameron said, the tiniest thread of little boy hurt lacing his voice. "Unlike you, I eat a lot and I like my food cholesterol laden. There's no need for you to pay for my vices."

Patricia stiffened at the mention of the word charity. "I wasn't going to let you starve," she snapped. "I just haven't had time to get to the grocery store. Thank you for saving me the trouble."

She lifted a sack out of the back of the pickup. "Let me get my checkbook and reimburse you."

Cameron shook his head, and a wayward shock of golden hair fell across his forehead. "There's no need. I charged the shingles to your account at the lumberyard. The food and the ladder are on me." His mouth twisted into a wry smile. "It is in my best interest after all to keep you from breaking your neck before payday rolls around."

Patricia's lips twitched. Darned if this contrary man didn't have a way of making her smile even when she was determined not to.

There was something different about the boss-lady this morning, but Cameron couldn't quite put his finger on it. Were her eyes somehow brighter, her cheeks redder, her lips pinker? He felt an unaccountable longing to loosen that glorious tumble of hair from the constraints of the rubber band which pulled it so severely away from her face. Instead he merely took the heavy sack of groceries from her.

"Let me get these."

It was not a request. Though tempted to tell him that she was used to carrying in her own groceries, Patricia acquiesced to his gallantry as meekly as one of the kittens frolicking on the lawn. She felt sorry for the poor creatures. Amy was wearing out the whole litter with her constant attention. Patricia bent down and cuddled one in her arms. It was Mittens, a white longhair born with two extra toes and a sweet, slightly goofy disposition. The creature purred contentedly in her mistress's arms.

"Thank you," she said to Cameron who looked so shocked by the simple statement that it made Patricia wonder, if like herself, he'd received too little by way of appreciation expressed in his life.

Feeling bad about having thought such rotten things about Cameron all morning, when in fact he had been out restocking her pantry, Patricia sorely regretted the cool reception she had given him. It was strange but nice having somebody fuss over her for a change.

"I'm glad you're back," she added, gracing him with her warmest smile.

"I'll warrant you won't be if you get back on that roof again," he growled.

Cameron had the oddest sensation that he had been sucker punched. The woman's gratitude turned him to mush. It was the most disconcerting feeling he'd ever encountered. One minute he wanted to throttle her and the next to discover if the passion smoldering in those sweet, chocolate-brown eyes extended all the way to her lips. If he was any judge of character, such a potential conflagration could level a forest fire in nothing flat. No telling what it could do to the dry kindling of a man's desire too long denied.

He made several trips back to the pickup while Patricia took the baby inside and began unloading the groceries. Steaks and roasts went into the freezer along with several tubs of expensive brand-name ice cream and a half dozen cartons of Popsicles she knew were purchased especially for the children. There were canned goods galore and lunch meats and fresh bread and sugar-sweetened cereals and tantalizing specialties from the local bakery that set Patricia's mouth watering.

She couldn't remember the last time she'd eaten any produce she hadn't grown herself, and the kids were sure to be in heaven gobbling the gobs of candy Cameron had bought. It had been a long time indeed since her shelves had been so full.

Once things were put away, Patricia insisted Cameron sit down and have a cup of coffee and one of the delectable cinnamon rolls he'd bought at the local bakery. No fancy flavored cappuccinos for Cameron Wade. He took his coffee just as Patricia suspected he would— black and hot enough to burn the top of one's mouth.

Watching the baby smear applesauce all over her face, Cameron laughed at the minuscule amount Amy actually managed to get into her mouth. His deep, rich voice filled the room and sent tremors sweeping through Patricia's insides. Despite the primitive warning signs rushing through her body, she could feel a palpable coziness to the scene. Through the fragrant steam rising from the cups sitting between them, she saw the flickering image of a real family in the amazing depths of Cameron's blue, blue eyes. And felt a curious longing.

The sound of a plastic bowl hitting the linoleum shattered the pleasant moment. Amy giggled in delight as applesauce flew everywhere, splattering the wallpaper, wrapping around the legs of the high chair and decorating the freshly scrubbed floor in the decor most favored by chimpanzees.

Reality was more scalding than the freshly brewed coffee Patricia had just poured into two cups. Daydreaming about a handsome knight rushing in on a white horse to save her from the drudgery of single motherhood was a waste of time she could ill afford. As her dour father had told Patricia more times than she could count, life was a series of choices.

She had made hers in direct opposition to his wishes, and according to Roland D'Winter it only served her right to have to lie in that proverbial bed. Not that he wouldn't welcome her back under his smothering control if she would only admit that she had been wrong and come back home as the penitent sinner. Trouble was, Patricia wasn't in the least contrite. No doubt about it, her life was hard. But it was her own, and it had made her strong. She was determined that her children would be raised in an atmosphere of love and encouragement. Unlike her own upbringing, they would grow up having faith in their ability to take whatever the world threw at them and make the best of it.

Patricia knew that it was not only useless to fantasize about life with a man who insisted on carrying in her groceries and thought roofing was masculine work, it was also unfair. To him. And to the children who would always come first in her life.

Despite predictions to the contrary, Patricia was proud of the fact that she was proving each and every day that a loving single mother was capable of taking care of her brood all by herself. Maybe her life had evolved into an unvarying hard routine, but that was no excuse to go around daydreaming about a virtual stranger. One who considered her as feather-brained as her livestock.

Patricia walked over to the sink to retrieve a sponge to clean up the mess and was surprised to hear herself ask, "Have you ever been married?"

Cameron snorted. "No, ma'am. Not me."

The conviction with which he uttered the words made Patricia smile.

"A confirmed bachelor, huh?"

"You could say that," he responded tersely.

He hadn't liked what he had glimpsed in Patricia's eyes a moment ago. Cameron had seen that same look before in dozens of other women's eyes. That hopeful, predatory look that always preceded the inevitable question about his marital status. It seemed to him that women were drawn to men who had never been married like hunters to a trophy buck. Proud of the fact that he had never been tagged, Cameron was determined to never have his head hanging over any woman's bed.

Nonetheless, his fortitude began to crumble as Patricia got down on her hands and knees and began swabbing up the sticky goo on the floor. His body responded involuntarily to the way her body moved as she worked. Swallowing the last gulp of hot coffee in one agonizing swig, he jumped up to go.

"Like you said, it's time I start earning my keep around here."

"I didn't mean it to sound like—"

The back door swung shut on the rest of Patricia's comment. A few minutes later over a sinkful of dirty dishes, she watched him haul her old ladder past the kitchen window and over to the woodpile—where he proceeded to chop it into kindling.

Patricia couldn't help but laugh out loud. He wasn't kidding about not wanting her back on that ladder. Or the roof either, for that matter, she realized as the sound of heavy footsteps overhead began resonating throughout the house.

Cameron's genuine concern for her well-being touched a chord deep inside of her. Why the last chivalrous man on the planet had somehow fallen on her doorstep, she wasn't sure, but Patricia wasn't above suspecting Hadley of intervening. Considering his lack of attention to their welfare when he had been with them on earth, it seemed the least he could do in the Hereafter was to send out a heavenly cavalry in the form of a big-hearted cowboy.

While Cameron was clomping around on the roof, Patricia took advantage of the rare opportunity to get caught up on her housework. It felt good to get at the inside work she'd been neglecting while focusing on more pressing outside jobs. Besides, she didn't want her new boarder to think her a slovenly landlady.

From his rooftop vantage point, Cameron had a bird's-eye view of a verdant valley surrounded by craggy mountain peaks. The only mark of humankind upon the panoramic scene was a lone red ribbon of road snaking its way through the clay of Red Canyon. Gazing upon the backside of creation, Cameron was convinced of the land's ability to withstand alteration. Like his grandfather before him, he vowed nothing would come between him and the land. He knew exactly what Spencer Wade had been thinking when he had so brazenly claimed this land as his own. Cameron's soul, too, was inexorably intertwined with this soil. Fate decreed that they would be buried together in the same hard-baked clay.

Looking down upon the maze of pens set up for the emus, Cameron was pleased to see how little space they actually took up. Long runways specifically designed to provide the birds with an avenue for great bursts of speed gave the silly critters ample opportunity to run up and down the length of chain-link fencing. As far as he could tell, they did nothing more than poop and run off what little meat was on their bones. Plucked, he'd be surprised to find more than a good-size turkey breast beneath all those feathers.

Soaking up the warm autumn sun, he visualized his own plans for this place. From his travels, he knew there was a crying need for quality quarter horses. With a little luck, a lucrative endorsement campaign, and a lot of hard work, he planned on making the Triple R synonymous with the finest horseflesh in the country. There was just one glitch in his well-laid plans: a headstrong brunette with a bewitching pair of eyes as changeable as springtime in Wyoming. At one moment they were soft, gentle and beguiling; the next, as cold and furious as a March blizzard.

A rusty rope of dust in the distance caught Cameron's eye. He checked his watch. It was almost four o'clock. That would be the school bus. The thought of seeing those two energetic little boys again twisted his lips into a smile. The wisp of a cloud passing overhead cast a thin shadow over his enthusiasm. Quickly, he reminded himself not to get overly involved in the comings and goings of this family. Particularly not when he was so intent on their going....

Chapter Five

Toting a baby on her hip and juggling a set of keys in one hand, Patricia checked her watch. She was running behind—as usual. Being a few minutes late to the bus stop might not have bothered most mothers, but the thought of having her children dropped off in the middle of the prairie made Patricia's heart beat as hard as a drill press. Despite repeated warnings about staying put and never taking up with strangers, she wouldn't put it past the boys to thumb a ride home without a second thought to their safety or her peace of mind. Likely they would treat any outsider as they had Cameron Wade—with more curiosity than concern.

As she crossed the yard, Patricia glanced up to see her new foreman hard at work. She sucked in her breath. Framed against a cerulean sky, the man was magnificent. He had abandoned his shirt to reveal a torso more rippled than the washboardy road that was systematically beating her vehicle to pieces. Haloed in sunlight his muscles glistened with sweat. For all intents and purposes it appeared as though a mythological god had alighted upon her roof. The crowbar he held could well have been a lightning bolt pointed directly at her heart.

She tripped over a loose rock in her path and heard Amy giggle at the thrill of being momentarily thrown off balance. Struggling to regain her footing, Patricia heard one of her father's favored sayings echoing in the corridors of her memory.

Keep your eyes on the ground and your head out of the clouds, girl!

She shook off the admonition with the same sense of resentment that it had evoked in her as a teen. It had been Patricia's father's Puritanical outlook on life that had propelled his daughter into the arms of a man more inclined to seeking fun and adventure than to earning his way into heaven through hard work and self-denial. After Hadley's death, Patricia defied her father again by refusing to abandon the ranch and move back to her parents' California home with its year-round sunshine and material comforts. Though the children's grandparents could certainly give them the monetary stability that had been so lacking in their young lives, the thought of their free spirits being crushed beneath the inflexibility that had permeated that old mausoleum in which she had been raised prevented Patricia from seriously considering it for more than two consecutive minutes.

Bound and determined to make a go of Hadley's Folly, as her father had dubbed the ranch, she squared her shoulders and vowed to continue putting one foot in front of the other.

One foot in front of the other, that was, as long as some perplexing blue-eyed drifter didn't go tripping her up. Patricia shifted the squirming bundle on her hip. As much as she would like to have believed that Amy had somehow made her stumble, she refused to lay blame falsely. The fact of the matter was that she'd been feeling off-kilter ever since Cameron Wade had blasted into her life with all the subtlety of a cyclone. Patricia's sense of light-headedness was compounded by the realization that he had somehow managed to strip the roof of more shingles in a few hours than she would have been able to in a week.

She was duly impressed. It would have taken even longer just to get Hadley to climb the ladder.

Oh, to have the strength of a man! Patricia thought wistfully to herself as she wrangled the baby into the car seat. If she only had the muscles to back her determination, there would have been no need to ever have placed the help-wanted ad that brought trouble to her doorstep wearing size-eleven cowboy boots and sporting an attitude to match. Her friendly wave goodbye to him came as more of a response to the unnerving feeling that Cameron was watching her every move with a mirthful eye than to any obligation to courtesy.

"I'll be back in a few," she called out more cheerfully than necessary just to show how little his bare chest bothered her.

His only response was a cursory nod of the head.

Cameron didn't bother hiding his fascination with Patricia's cute little wiggle as she hopped into that old rattletrap of hers and disappeared over the hill. The pickup was soon obliterated by clouds of dust, leaving him with the eerie sense of being the only person left on Earth. He was familiar with that lonesome feeling, had in fact armed himself with it as a young man out to make a name and grown to like it in the process. A loner, he reveled in the solitude of mountain vistas and

the canvas of a cloudless Wyoming sky unmarred by
man's heavy hand. Cooped up in the hospital for an
extended period, he had longed for fresh air and freedom and the chance to be in control of his life again.
The pure simplicity of manual labor was more thera-
peutic than anything a doctor could prescribe. As far as
he was concerned, not even the glamour and excitement
of the rodeo scene could compete with the satisfaction
a man got from working on his own place. And despite
what any registered deed said, in Cameron's mind this
ranch was already as good as his. From his lofty perch
he felt the master of all he could survey. The lord of
foreverness in every direction.

    "Hey, Cameron!"
    "We're home!"
Two little boys spilled out of the truck that had just
barely jerked to a dusty stop in the driveway. Jolted
from pensive reflections by their hollering, Cameron
wondered what it would feel like to receive such a
hearty welcome every day. An empty motel room sure
as heck couldn't compete with the look of genuine excitement upon these children's open faces.
    He dismissed the odd twist in his chest with a glance
at the pail of dirty diapers sitting on the edge of the
porch. What man in his right mind would willingly
exchange his independence for a ready-made family?
For desultory obligations, endless bills and inescapable
henpecking? The very thought sent a shiver up his
spine. After years of being nailed shut, his heart wasn't
about to be pried open with anything as maudlin as
cheap sentimentality. The one time he'd opened himself
to the possibility of falling in love, Bonnie had stabbed
him in the back with less compunction than Brutus had

Julius Caesar. With a deft twist of the wrist, Cameron tore loose a section of shingling, leaving the naked wood beneath exposed to the sudden light of day.

Johnny dashed into the barn as fast as a jack rabbit and returned a minute later, dragging an old, frayed piece of clothesline behind him. Cameron grinned. The little cuss was going to hold him to the offhanded promise he'd exacted last night about showing him how to work a lasso.

"Chores first," Patricia called out before he had gotten halfway across the front lawn.

"Aw, Mom!" both boys cried simultaneously.

Steeling herself against a barrage of whining, Patricia grabbed her youngest by the hand before she could take off after her big brothers.

"Play?" Amy inquired over the fist she was attempting to stick into her mouth.

"No play," her mother replied with a weariness that bespoke just how tired she really was. The fatigue seemed to have settled deep into her bones and was mirrored in her eyes as she led the girl out of harm's way.

"Go on and do as your mother says now," Cameron instructed the boys as he made his way down the ladder. "Maybe there'll be time afterward for me to show you a rope trick or two."

The effect his words had upon Johnny and Kirk was nothing short of amazing. Patricia noted wryly how their objections ceased immediately. Cameron's unexpected support was a nice change from Hadley's general ambivalence. Only too happy to allow the children free rein with their imaginations, their father had shrunk from enforcing rules, setting deadlines and adhering to the mundane strictures of everyday living. Though Patricia hated always being the heavy in the family, she had learned early on in their marriage that trying to change her husband was like trying to change the direction of the fickle Wyoming wind. Instead she tried to focus on Hadley's good points.

While he may not have been the most responsible parent in the world, Hadley Erhart had been able to find the fun in life. Chores never had come first with him...or even second or third. And as much as Patricia had resented that when he was alive, she found it was what she missed most about him now that he was gone. Without his happy-go-lucky influence to lighten the burden of daily obligations, she often felt more like a boot camp sergeant than a mother.

As she hustled about the kitchen preparing their supper, Patricia couldn't help dwelling upon the fact that the boys hadn't so much as questioned Cameron's directive to do their chores. While happy to avoid what had become a daily battle with her children, she also felt a disturbing sense of foreboding. Apparently any male role model had the power to make a big impression on Johnny and Kirk. Even a temporary one bound to them by nothing more than a piece of paper and a questionable sense of duty.

Cameron shook his head over the frazzled cord Johnny had thrust into his hands before rushing off to complete his chores. It seemed symbolic of this raggle-taggle family and their tenuous hold upon this ranch. He suspected that the slightest stress would likely cause it to snap in two. Not stopping to contemplate why his heart was choking him, he walked over to his pickup with purposeful strides. He couldn't very well teach the boys how to rope without the proper equipment now could he? Though he had not had the huge success with it that he had with bull riding, Cameron was no stranger to steer roping. Pulling his own rope from behind the seat, he proceeded to twirl it over his head a couple of times before sending it whirling through the air like a writhing white snake. It landed neatly over his target— a corner post of the corral.

A self-satisfied smile curled his lip. While it wasn't exactly his intention to impress the boys with a demonstration of his cowboy prowess, he didn't particularly want to embarrass himself in front of them, either. He figured showing those twin tornadoes the basic techniques of roping and having them practice on their own, would be a surefire way of keeping them out of his hair for a while. After all, it would be a whole lot easier attending to the business at hand if he didn't have a couple of pint-size fans dogging his heels every second of the day. Fans, he reminded himself, who could easily be crushed if he wasn't careful about watching his step around them.

An old sawhorse had been set up in the corral, and Patricia noted with amusement that someone had attached a set of horns to it. The rope Cameron was handling could well have been her heartstrings. She felt its certain tug as it sailed over its mark. What she would have given for her husband to have spent more of his time on earth engaging in such quality time with their boys. Unfortunately Hadley had been so engrossed in moneymaking schemes that he'd been generally oblivious to his sons' desperate bids for their father's attention. Presently they were flanking Cameron on either side, hanging on his every word. Patricia was surprised they weren't taking notes.

With an expert flick of the wrist, her foreman removed the lasso from the stationary bull without budging an inch from his perch.

"Your turn to give it a try," he said, handing Johnny the rope.

The boy's first attempt was a dismal failure underscored by the sound of his little brother's loud guffaw. Patricia readied herself to intervene in a typical display of sibling rivalry, but whatever Cameron said to them too quietly for her to overhear rendered her good intentions unnecessary. They suddenly erupted into a gale of giggles.

The sound of their laughter seeped into Patricia's chest, making her breath come in shallow sips. Darn it, the last thing she needed right now was for the boys to bond with some drifter who was loath to making a measly three-month commitment. Considering how disappointed they were when he hadn't shown up for breakfast this morning, Patricia knew she was witnessing an emotional disaster in the making.

That knowledge did not stop her, however, from admiring the view. Those three denim-clad bottoms perched atop her corral gate would have made an adorable postcard. The one in the middle would have singularly made a great beefcake pinup. Of course, she wasn't into that sort of thing, Patricia primly reminded herself. As a mother of three, she was far too mature to indulge in such girlish flights of fancy.

Nonetheless, there was no telling how long her gaze might have remained affixed to Cameron's fine-looking derriere had not a surprised hoot suddenly gone up from the spectators sitting on the fence. A second later the panicky sound of an emu grunting in distress sent Patricia bounding to the rescue.

"Whoaaaa!" screamed Kirk.

"Let go of the rope!" hollered Cameron as Johnny went flying off the gate.

"Aaaaaaaaahhhh!" he cried in midair before hitting the ground so hard it sounded like it ought to bust wide open from the impact.

The boy sat looking bewildered in the midst of a billow of dust, which hadn't so much as settled before Patricia was over the gate and gathering her little angel into her arms.

"Are you hurt?" she asked.

Tears welled up in his eyes. Looking from his mother to the big man wearing the black cowboy hat, he blinked back his tears.

"I'm okay," he sniffled, pulling away in obvious embarrassment.

The fear that held Patricia's heart captive released its viselike grip, and she felt her blood beginning to pump again in steady, angry beats.

"What in the world did you think you were doing?" she demanded, pulling her son to his feet and checking him over for broken bones.

Knowing full well that the question was not directed at a hapless ten-year-old but rather a grown man who should have known better than to come between a mama bear and her cubs, Cameron rubbed his chin thoughtfully before interrupting Johnny's halting explanation.

"I've never seen anything like it. Darned if one of those fool birds of yours didn't run under the lasso just as it was settling where Johnny was aiming—right at that old sawhorse."

The look on Johnny's face spoke volumes in gratitude.

Patricia glowered up at Cameron. Neither the lie nor the complicity sat well with her. Instilling a sense of uncompromising honesty in her boys was of utmost concern to her. Unlike their father, she was determined to root her children solidly in reality.

"Am I supposed to buy that line of malarkey?"

"Uh-huh."

Unable to recognize a rhetorical question for what it was, Kirk helpfully responded, then stepped away from his mother's dirty look in confusion.

Dusting Johnny off with an experienced hand, Patricia turned a dangerously soft voice upon Cameron. He was reminded of the deceptive calm just before the chute was opened and a ton of angry bull exploded into the arena.

"And I suppose *you* didn't have any idea that the boys wouldn't be satisfied with just roping inanimate objects?"

"I sure wasn't when I was his age," Cameron admitted with a cocky smile that Patricia suspected had been perfected at a tender age to get him out of similar scrapes with his own mother. After all, what woman wouldn't weaken under the power of matching dimples, twinkling eyes and a voice so rich and deep it could qualify as a purr?

Patricia mentally supplied the answer to her own question. One concerned about her son breaking his neck while under this stranger's questionable tutelage, that's who.

"Johnny could have been seriously injured," she reminded him. "Do you have any idea how far it is to the local hospital?"

A disparaging sound rose from the back of Cameron's throat. He resented being treated like some asphalt cowboy who didn't know his hind end from his hat. Did *he* know? How well he remembered those trips to the emergency room: bleeding into wet towels as he mentally prepared himself for being stitched up like Raggedy Andy, cradling a broken arm against his chest while assuring his mother each agonizing mile that he was going to be all right. As a boy Cameron had played hard. Things hadn't changed much since he'd reached manhood—except that now he played for keeps.

"I'd wager his pride is hurt worse than anything else," he offered philosophically and turning to both boys added with a wink. "Before you know it, not only will you be roping those contrary critters but breaking 'em as well."

The comment had been made in jest, but Patricia was far from amused. Her boys were highly susceptible to any suggestions that centered on playing cowboy, and visions of one calamity after another danced before her mind's eye.

"That's all I need—to have to put down perfectly healthy livestock because you're playing rodeo with my boys. In case you aren't aware, emus are like horses in a number of ways. Most notable if they break a leg, there's nothing to do but put them out of their misery. An expensive proposition that I can hardly afford."

"Playing rodeo!"

Patricia's words drilled him between the eyes with the force of a mule's kick. Had she been a man, he'd have expressed his outrage with his fists. "Do you have the faintest idea who you're talking to?"

Amused by his injured tone of voice, she responded coolly. "My foreman. I believe that I'm telling my foreman to stop endangering my children and my stock."

"Calling those overgrown dodos stock is like calling

that stick horse over there a registered stud." He gestured toward a broomstick horse propped forlornly against the corral fence. Patricia had lovingly fashioned him as a Christmas gift one year. It hung its cloth head in embarrassment.

The slur acted as a fan to a flicker of pride sheltered deep inside Patricia's heart that refused to be blown out despite her husband's death, her father's condemnation, the disdain of her neighbors—and the palatable scorn of her hired man.

"I'd appreciate it if you wouldn't take out your prejudices upon my *stock*. And that means no roping, choking, riding or belittling them in front of my children!"

Patricia's insistence upon referring to those miserable birds as legitimate stock unleashed Cameron's ire. No matter how intriguing those dark eyes were when flashing like opals with the fire of self-righteous determination, the woman was pushing her luck. He'd have her know that he was not the type of man to take guff from anyone.

"Rest assured, honey, I'm not tempted in the least to throw a saddle on some bucking bird! Chicken rodeo isn't my style."

The sexist endearment had clearly been intended to rile her. It worked only too well. Though Patricia had never slapped a man before, nothing at the moment would have given her more satisfaction than to smack this one clear into next week.

"Honey," she mimicked, "you can take that stick horse over there and put it—"

"Have you ever been in a real rodeo?" Johnny interrupted, his eyes wide with awe.

Cameron did not shift his gaze from Patricia's flushed face. For some reason he took perverse pleasure in ruffling her feathers. Maybe it was because so few women had ever stood up to him the way this spirited little spitfire did. Generally women liked being on his good side, preferably for a profile shot in some flashy rag.

"A few," he admitted with a self-effacing shrug.

"Ever win anything?" Kirk wanted to know.

"You could say that."

Fascinated beyond belief, the boys began shooting questions at him in rapid machine-gun style.

Patricia cringed at the matching looks of adulation upon her sons' faces. She hadn't been married long before discovering that most of Hadley's supposed accomplishments were nothing more than figments of his overactive imagination.

She raised a questioning eyebrow at Cameron's evasive responses to her son's inquiries. He hadn't initially struck her as one given to prevaricating, but a man's ego was a strange and unpredictable thing.

"And just what is it you've won? A race around the barrels on some world-famous Thoroughbred?"

Thunder passed over Cameron's face. There was no way to interpret that jab other than as a direct insult to his masculinity. Even the greenest dude knew that barrel racing was a woman's event.

He took a step toward her, coming so close that she could actually feel his breath warm upon her cheek. Patricia smelled his scent. The hint of cologne blended with honest sweat forming a musky fragrance that made her head swim.

He towered over her. Glaring.

And all she could focus on was the way his mouth looked so firm and inviting beneath that sexy mustache. Would that he would punish her for mocking him with a kiss!

"I'll have you know," he growled. "I just so happen to have won a national title and I've got the trophy buckle to prove it."

Up until now, Patricia had been too focused on her primitive reaction to the man to pay much attention to his words. When the absurdity of his claim finally penetrated the sweet fog surrounding her brain, she laughed out loud. She'd heard enough of Hadley's tall tales to recognize this one as a real beaut.

"Sure, sure you have," she said, playing along in exaggerated tones and flicking the brim of his hat. "And I bet you paid a bundle for it at the pawn shop. Does it match that ten-gallon hat attitude of yours? Gosh, how embarrassing for a man of your stature to be working here of all places on an emu ranch. How humbling!"

Cameron snapped his mouth shut over the expletive blistering the roof of his mouth. Had a man thrown such a sucker punch his way, he'd have lit into him with the force of a freight train.

"Hey, if it's any consolation, I had a heck of a time myself selecting you from among all those other rodeo stars who applied for this job—and the movie stars, too."

The risk of being stomped into oblivion before thousands of voyeurs was nothing compared to the pain of hearing Patricia's laughter directed at him. The sound wrapped itself around his heart like barbed wire. The fact that she didn't believe him evoked a flood of bitter memories of all those who'd had no faith in the power of his dreams.

His blue eyes narrowed. Never in a thousand years would he have taken this sweet-faced mommy for the kind who finds a debilitating shot to a man's crotch on those stupid home video shows the height of hilarity, but the sound of her tinkling laughter confirmed it. He was working for a closet castrater. Of course, he suspected that in their secret hearts all women were. Bonnie sure as heck had been.

His eyes took on a steely glint. His jaw a proud set.

"Go ahead and laugh," he told her, hurt that she neither recognized nor believed him.

Up on the roof he'd had a weak moment and actually considered coming clean about his covert plan to buy her out, but her barbed jeers cinched it, but good. As far as he was concerned, it would serve Patricia Erhart right to lose the whole damned ranch for nothing more than back taxes.

Just wait and see who had the last laugh.

Chapter Six

Still fuming about the razzing Patricia had given him earlier, Cameron swaggered up to the dinner table like a bear with a sore paw. He looked fully prepared to take up where they had left off—back at the Showdown at the EMU Corral. To his surprise, however, his hostess merely smiled as pretty as you please and asked him how he liked his steak cooked.

"Rare."

Thinking he looked as if he could eat it raw, Patricia chirped back in her best imitation of a short-order cook, "Coming right up!"

She was truly sorry about hurting her foreman's feelings. After all, if the man felt the need to embellish his life with preposterous claims to fame, the least she could do was nod politely and feign belief. Unfortunately, after a lifetime of watching her husband color his world with broad strokes from the most flattering palette, Patricia had become hardened to such "harmless" lies. She hadn't been married long before discovering, just as her father had warned her, that most of Hadley's supposed accomplishments were little more than figments of an overactive imagination. He maintained it was a result of kissing the Blarney Stone, but that too was fabrication. The closest Hadley had come to Ireland was Patrick O'Hara's Corner Bar and Grill.

Perhaps that was at the heart of why Patricia couldn't make herself believe Cameron's outlandish claims. Whether he knew it or not, the man was already proving to have significant impact on her boys. She didn't want them growing up believing, as their father had, that the ability to spin a good yarn could surpass hard work and a solid education in getting them where they needed to be in the twenty-first century.

Still she felt a twinge of guilt about being responsible for that injured-puppy-dog look still lingering on Cameron's face. Hopefully a nice meal would help assuage his wounded pride.

"Here you go," she said, setting his plate before him with a flourish.

Simmering in a puddle of pink juices, the thick steak was cooked just the way he liked it—barely warm. Beside it sat a baked potato heaped with sour cream. Despite his resolve to stay mad, Cameron felt his ill temper beginning to melt like the pats of butter atop a pyramid of home-made biscuits Patricia stacked before him.

"Funny," he said, devouring one in two bites. "I had you figured strictly as a granola cruncher. Didn't think I'd ever be privileged to this much cholesterol at one sitting."

"A hard-working man deserves a good meal, and you don't exactly strike me as the type to be satisfied with just a big, old salad."

The simple acknowledgment of his work touched a

cold spot deep inside Cameron. His initial disappointment at not being able to rile her was offset by the pull
of a smile that was as heady and sweet as wine—and
just as addictive, he feared. He studied Patricia thoughtfully as she buzzed about the kitchen. She had changed
into a faded pair of blue jeans and a pink, fuzzy sweater.
The effect was a decided improvement over those baggy
overalls she favored. Why a woman built like her
wanted to cover up all those luscious curves was beyond
him. Did she know she looked as mouthwatering as
anything on his plate?

He was reminded of a hummingbird as Patricia flitted
from one task to another: prompting them to say the
evening blessing, pouring the milk, mashing up the
baby's potato with a lightning-fast fork, handing out
extra napkins and refilling the saltshaker. Her move-
ments were graceful and efficient.

Just watching her made him wonder aloud, "Do *you*
ever get to eat a warm meal?"

Patricia thought it an odd question. One Hadley
would never have thought to ask her. "I can't remember
one," she replied honestly.

As she brushed aside a stray lock of hair in a gesture
that bespoke her weariness, Cameron felt an odd longing to test the silkiness of that unruly strand between
his own rough fingers. His mouth curved in a lazy
smile.

"You know," he chided gently, "with the exception
of the little one in the high chair, I'd wager the rest of
us are perfectly capable of taking care of ourselves. Isn't
that right, boys?"

Pleased to be consulted in such a grown-up manner,
they nodded their heads enthusiastically. Of course. Pa-

tricia thought they probably would have agreed to eat a rattlesnake if Cameron suggested it.

"Why don't you sit down and enjoy your food with the rest of us?"

Part of Patricia longed to submit to his perfectly logical suggestion. And part warned her to stay well out of striking distance of that killer smile. Deciding it was impossible to feel comfortable beneath Cameron's potent scrutiny, she self-consciously untied the apron around her waist and draped it over the back of her chair. The tired, old scrap of material looked the way she felt—far more serviceable than sexy.

Just as she was settling herself into her seat, Johnny blurted out, "What did you do in the rodeo, Cameron?"

"Bronco busting?" asked Kirk, his wide eyes reflecting his admiration.

"Bull doggin'?" his brother persisted. "Calf ropin'?"

Patricia found it easier to cut through the steak on her plate than the tension that suddenly filled the air. She swallowed with difficulty and pointedly glared at both boys, foolishly hoping that they would take her cue and drop the subject.

"Bull riding," Cameron replied tersely, tossing daggers in Patricia's direction.

It was all she could do not to roll her eyes. Of course, he would pick the most dangerous event to impress the boys.

"Wow!" Johnny exclaimed. "And you're a national champ—?"

"Save room for cake," Patricia interrupted, "before you get filled up with a bunch—of other stuff that might be hard to digest."

Cameron's knife clattered onto his plate.

"Like a diet of crow?" he asked, burning a hole right through her with his piercing blue eyes.

"Chocolate cake?" Kirk interrupted, blissfully ignorant of the strain between the two adults.

Patricia nodded. "Double fudge."

"Devil's food, I'd wager," Cameron interjected, feeling sure it would have to be the color of the eyes that mocked him. And just as tempting.

"I made it in your honor," Patricia replied in a saccharine tone as she sashayed out of the room.

She didn't bother asking if he wanted any, just returned a moment later with a huge slice of deep dark chocolate cake topped with a generous scoop of vanilla ice cream. Her eyes were too bright to be trusted as she shoved it in front of him.

A traitorous stomach overruled injured pride. What man could resist such sinful goodness? It took only one bite for Cameron to succumb to one of the primal forces of nature—chocolate.

Taking a long look at the vision in pink before him, he mumbled through a mouthful of calories, "Heaven."

He just couldn't seem to stay mad at a woman who stood her ground with such moxy. The truth of the matter was he liked the lady's sass. In his lifetime, Cameron had met few people who could give back just as good as he gave out. Men were afraid of his fists. Buckle bunnies just wanted in his pants and his wallet, never daring to counter anything he said, no matter how ridiculous. Bonnie's loose lips had been better at kissing his supposed friends than providing stimulating conversation. Seldom was Cameron given the opportunity for the kind of verbal sparring that Patricia threw his way. Finding it oddly arousing, he wondered how many married couples engaged in such skirmishes as a form of foreplay. His mind traveled the short distance to the woman sitting across the table from him and—

"If you wouldn't mind helping with dishes again tonight, I'd like to have a talk with you."

Shaken from his mutinous thoughts by the unexpected request, Cameron hoped the lady wasn't a mind reader. Not that she had to be when he'd been so blatant about looking at her like that decadent piece of cake he'd devoured in all of three bites.

"Sure," he replied in a tone of forced nonchalance.

"You boys are excused from the table," their mother told them. "Just take your plates to the sink when you're done and get started on your homework right away. You can work in the living room."

Johnny and Kirk needed no encouragement to escape the drudgery of doing dishes. They were out of the room faster than Cameron could blink. Oblivious to her brothers' hasty departure from the dinner table, Amy was up to her elbows in chocolate cake. She appeared to be decorating herself with it. It was in her hair, smeared all over her face, and dangling like earrings from her small lobes. Two green eyes peered at Cameron behind a nut-brown mask.

He ventured an observation. "She looks like Curious George."

It struck Patricia funny that this rough-and-tumble cowboy had referenced back to one of her children's favorite stories. She giggled at the image.

"I've called her a little monkey more than once myself," she admitted. "If you don't mind, I think I'll just let her enjoy her food for a little while. That way you and I can talk in peace before World War III erupts when I try giving her a bath."

Cameron not only saw the logic in her reasoning, but

also admired it. He detested persnickety mothers who followed after their children with dustpans and wash-cloths, ever ready to attack every crumb. Never allow-ing a moment of dirt and fun, it seemed to him that they were constantly scolding their charges for any childish play. He supposed such children grew up to be fine accountants and lawyers but doubted whether any stood a chance at becoming anything as undomesticated as a cowboy.

Clearing the table in silence, he wondered what Pa-tricia had to say that she didn't want the boys to hear. Was he going to receive his walking papers? Or pos-sibly an apology for calling him a liar in front of the children?

As she filled the sink with sudsy water, he assumed his position as drier. Cameron's mind went back to a time long ago when he had come down the stairs in this very house and accidentally overheard his parents' pri-vate conversation. Early risers, they shared their morn-ing offering and daily concerns out of their children's earshot. It had been a sacred time, given to the rituals of lifetime lovers. Hot coffee, sweet, unhurried kisses, and a view through the front window of the sun rising like a fierce gladiator, spreading its dazzling morning cloak upon a cold earth.

"It's over, Rose. I've lost it all." Cameron heard his father's voice crack with emotion.

"You haven't lost me." Rose Wade wrapped her arms around him as if he were one of her children in need of a hug and a bandage. *"You can never lose this family's love or respect."*

Cameron's throat closed around the memory. No child should ever have to witness his hero lose self-respect. From that day forward he came to understand just how different the outside world was from this cozy kitchen with its cheerful wallpaper and homespun rugs. Standing on the threshold of his memories, he felt a fierce desire to recoup that elusive sense of security he had taken for granted for the first decade of his life.

If he could but buy it back, he intended to make it his for life.

"What was it you wanted to talk to me about?" he asked in a tone that was inexplicably gruff.

"I want to ask you a...a...favor."

Forcing her eyes from the safety of gentle suds to the dangerous territory of Cameron's piercing blue gaze, she groped for the right words. Tactful honesty was what was called for.

"You must know that my boys are very vulnerable right now. They're looking for a male role model, and I'm worried they'll just latch on to the first one to saunter into their lives."

"And I'm the lucky guy." Cameron's laugh was dry. "Let me guess—you think I'm setting a bad example for your children. Is that it?"

Patricia had hoped to avoid phrasing it quite so bluntly.

"Not exactly," she stammered, wishing there was some way of explaining without giving a piece of her heart away in the process. "You see, their father was a good man. He just wasn't completely—" she searched for the kindest word "—honest with them...or with himself for that matter."

Cameron put his dishtowel down and gave Patricia the benefit of his full attention. "What do you mean?"

"I mean he was given to...flights of fancy."

Reading the perplexed expression on Cameron's face,

she made herself go on. As painful as this was for her, it had to be said. For the children's sake, if not her own.

"That is to say he exaggerated. Stretched the truth. Lied…" There she had said it at last. "In order to make himself look bigger in his boys' eyes."

When Cameron remained silent, she plunged ruthlessly onward, hating herself for betraying her husband's memory. "I must have told him a thousand times that he didn't need to. We loved him for who he was. A kind man. A funny man. A dreamer who was never meant for a world as grim as this one."

Patricia damned the tears glistening in her eyes. She wouldn't cry. She wouldn't. Wouldn't.

A single tear rolled down her cheek.

"The point is I'm very sensitive to anything that smacks of a falsehood—no matter how well intended. How seemingly innocent."

"You really don't believe a word I told you, do you?"

As hard as it was to overlook his injured tone of voice, Patricia could not back away from the truth. "Why would a rodeo star work for peanuts?" she asked.

Cameron resented the troubled look in those soft brown eyes. Sigmund Freud could not have looked more sympathetic to his plight as a compulsive liar. He raged against the injustice of her unfounded assumptions. He was half tempted to resurrect the silver and gold championship belt buckle that he had packed away, and shove it in her face. Of course, such rash behavior would indeed pique her curiosity as to why he actually had signed on as her hired hand. The timing for divulging that information just wasn't quite right. He hadn't made up his mind just how he was going to pull this off yet. It would be far better to just let Patricia find out on her own just how wrong she was. He hoped he had the satisfaction of being there when it happened, and in a community as small as theirs, it was bound to—sooner or later. The frosting on the proverbial devil's food cake would be her humble, and hopefully public, apology.

"Fine," he said flatly.

"You have to understand," Patricia continued, stricken by the stony expression upon her foreman's face, "that I'm thinking of you, as well."

His silence spoke louder than words.

"I'd hate for anything bad to happen to you just because I was afraid to confront you. You see, I'm partially responsible for my husband's death."

She wanted to explain how because she had loved Hadley she had protected him as best she could from reality. Had lied and covered up for him on occasions too numerous to count.

Released from the secret caverns of her heart, the spoken words were covered in her husband's blood. Cameron was looking at her like she was a crazy woman who just might pull a knife from the soapsuds and plunge it into his heart without compunction.

"You don't understand," she whispered. "It's not what you're thinking. I was his enabler."

While confined to a hospital bed, Cameron had watched his fair share of hit-and-run psychiatrists on daytime talk shows, and he had something to say on the matter. How long had this poor woman been blaming herself for circumstances out of her control?

"If you ask me, that's just a fancy name for somebody nice."

"Or a euphemism for a murderer." Patricia's voice

was as flat as a death knell. "If only I had been strong enough to help Hadley face his weaknesses instead of always covering for him, maybe my children wouldn't be without a father. If only I wouldn't have allowed him out on such a snowy night... I should have known he would head to the bar and would insist on driving home despite the roads being so treacherous."

Expecting Cameron to back away from her in horror now that he knew the truth about her, Patricia focused on the hint of gray in his mustache and the unforgiving lines of the mouth it sheltered. She awaited his condemnation with her back ramrod straight, subconsciously welcoming it as her due.

But Cameron did not back away. Instead he stepped forward and wrapped her as gently in his arms as he would any wounded creature. And when she tilted her face to his and searched his eyes in bewilderment, he traced with his thumb the track that solitary tear had left upon her cheek. Her heart leaped at the intimacy of the gesture, its wild beat striking against his own, pounding out a savage song of fear—and need.

"Honey, you might as well blame the barkeep who served him more than the legal limit allowed," he murmured softly into her ear. A sense of protectiveness unlike anything he'd ever felt before corkscrewed through his body. Her hair was soft against his cheek and smelled of sweet spices. He breathed deeply of her fragrance, reveling in the perfect fit of her body to his. An angel, she wanted nothing more of him than simple compassion and understanding.

"But we both know that wouldn't be right, either. Nobody forced alcohol down your husband's throat that night he went and got himself killed. Each of us is responsible for our own destiny. And each of us has our own reasons for doing what we do.''

His words were heavy with double meaning. When Patricia discovered the real reason he'd signed on, he doubted she would be as forgiving of him as she had of the husband who had not deserved her devotion. Her honesty was too brutal to bear. It was like looking directly into the sun. It burned an image onto the retina that was permanent.

His arms fell loosely to his side, and he took a deliberate step back.

Patricia was as moved by Cameron's sudden gentleness toward her as she was startled by his abrupt withdrawal. "You're right, of course," she murmured. "Each of us has our own reasons for what we do."

The sound of roughhousing in the next room vibrated throughout the house, a loud reminder of why she would continue her fight against all odds. Patricia was glad of the diversion. It helped her shake off a mood too somber. After all, the possibility of romance with this drifter whose arms had gone around her in comfort was almost as ludicrous as pretending there was anything more permanent between them than a wrinkled contract.

She understood Cameron's need to revisit his childhood home, but it was dangerous to consider his pilgrimage as anything more than the temporary desire to re-experience his youth. After all, a man as good as Cameron was with his hands and his head and his heart wasn't likely to remain a drifter long. Some nice, unattached woman without a ready-made family was bound to snatch him up and find a permanent spot for his boots under her bed.

Patricia felt a painful twinge in her chest at the

thought. As attached to his grandfather's legacy as Cameron seemed, she wouldn't be surprised if he wasn't secretly hoping to buy the ranch back someday and start his own family here. Unfortunately the cost of nostalgia didn't come cheap, and even if he could scrounge up the money somehow, Patricia wasn't interested in selling.

She did not reprimand her boys for making too much noise. To her, their laughter was the sound of healing in its purest form. Unlike the elegant museum her father had designed to impress the world, she loved this old house for the humble way it absorbed a family's bumps and bruises and made them its own. The notches on the kitchen door that marked the presence of a previous generation were now joined by her own children's as a visual reminder to her that life goes on.

Chapter Seven

At midnight, Cameron opened one unfriendly eye and checked the clock ticking on his nightstand. Annoyed to discover that he'd been lying awake for the better part of two hours, he rolled over and punched his pillow, determined not to lose another precious minute of sleep. After staring at the ceiling for an interminable length of time, he finally drifted off only to be taunted in his dreams by a collage of confusing images. Standing in the midst of an empty arena, he bowed to the sound of laughter. An old man with a Colt .45 commanded him to make a man of himself. Wearing a crown that proclaimed her official queen of the buckle bunnies, Bonnie winked at him behind a kissing booth where a string of acquaintances awaited their turn. Two boys dressed in old-time Western wear held him hostage with nothing more than their index fingers, and an angel in a pink angora sweater and skintight jeans beckoned him with outstretched arms and pursed lips.

She looked achingly familiar.

Bathed in a sheen of sweat, Cameron awoke with a mouth full of goose down pillow.

He arose a few short hours later wondering how he was going to face himself in the mirror. Patricia's tender display of vulnerability yesterday had left him unsettled and sexually frustrated. Though he had long ago realized that buckle bunnies could never fulfill his deeper psychological need for closeness and intellectual stimulation, Cameron couldn't deny the fact that there was a decided void in his life that only a woman could fulfill.

The fact that he wasn't willing to make a commitment to anyone complicated matters. Bonnie's infidelity had hurt him deeply. Perhaps less because of any real emotional attachment he had felt than the fact that she had so blatantly used him. As long as he was winning, all was lovey-dovey. But two summers ago when he'd hit a slump, Bonnie had turned as nippy toward him as a northern gale just before it dumps six feet of snow. Before Cameron knew what hit him, she had taken up with one of his old buddies who just happened to be having better luck in the arena than he. A bull goring him with both horns and trampling him to mincemeat beneath his hooves couldn't have inflicted more damage to Cameron's ego. The experience left him as wary as a wolf.

The thought of rubbing Bonnie's upturned nose in a nationally televised win was only part of what motivated him to tape up the ribs he had broken in semifinals and risk his life for a championship buckle. A buckle that would help him reclaim his heritage and his pride. A buckle that was going to make a lifelong dream an eventuality.

Still no hunk of metal, regardless of how big or pres-

tigious, could keep him warm at night, and Cameron's
thoughts turned again to the luscious creature who had
tempted him in his dreams. Since lying in bed was getting him nowhere fast, he struggled out of his blankets,
hoping that a hot cup of coffee and a cool shower would
put those haunting images out of his mind.

Against the first weak light of day, the ranch house
looked silent, dark and curiously inviting. As a child,
he had always liked the thought of being the first up in
the morning and relished opening the day like a shiny
gift-wrapped package. Dawn in the high country was
growing chillier with the approach of winter. A man
who liked to sleep in the nude, Cameron was spurred
into action by the nip of cold air on bare flesh. He
slipped into his work clothes and pulled on his boots
with an efficiency of movement that gave little indication of the permanent ache that had settled into bones
and joints too long abused by hard living. A moment
later he was out the door and unintentionally rousing a
couple of emus from their sleep as he passed by the
corral. Tossing a rude gesture in their general vicinity,
he stole into the main house as silently as a burglar.

Funny how after all these years he could still remember every creak in the floorboards. Not wanting to wake
his parents on their only day to sleep in, Cameron had
memorized the chronic ills of this house on his weekly
trek to watch Sunday morning cartoons on their old
black-and-white set. Tiptoeing over each woody chirp
brought back a sense of déjà vu so intense as to make
him pause in mid-step to consider it.

He found himself standing in front of the bedroom
that had been his parents'. It was Patricia's room now.
The door stood ajar, and he assumed she had left it open
out of necessity in case the baby cried out.

As Cameron gazed into the room, his breath caught in his lungs. He felt a sharp, masculine reaction at the nearness of the sleeping figure on the bed. She was beautiful. Wrapped in a floral sheet like a butterfly escaping its sweet cocoon of sleep, the woman was a vision any artist would long to capture on canvas. Her chestnut-colored hair was spread like a curtain of deep satin upon her pillow. A hint of lace caressed white shoulders. Untouched by any cosmetic attempts to improve perfection, she seemed a goddess, ethereal and radiant in the first rays of the sun spilling through her window. Cameron found the simple cotton gown she wore more alluring than any expensive negligee made for the express purpose of driving a man wild.

Feeling suddenly a voyeur, he wondered how he would possibly explain himself if for some inexplicable reason Sleeping Beauty were to awaken and discover him gawking at her. He forced his feet to move on, but neither a sense of guilt nor self-will could compel his mind to relinquish the erotic image that made the need for his shower to be a very cold one.

Patricia was not a morning person. Never had been. No matter how early she went to bed the night before, daybreak always arrived too soon. She slapped her alarm clock as if holding it personally responsible for bringing on the day before she was ready for it. Moaning, she burrowed deeper into the warmth of her bedcovers. Heaven, she had decided long ago, would be the luxury of an entire unplanned morning to languish in bed.

Unfortunately motherhood was not conducive to the fulfillment of such fantasies. She knew too well that if she didn't drag herself out of bed right now, her chances

of getting a shower were nil. Any minute now the baby
would be clamoring for breakfast, an ordeal certain to
be followed by the agony of trying to awaken Kirk. The
lad had his mother's grumpy, morning disposition, and
the two of them clashing over a bowl of oatmeal wasn't
a pretty sight. Undoubtedly in the midst of breakfast
Johnny would remember a crucial piece of homework
that he had neglected to do and would demand his
mother's undivided attention. As if his brother and sister
were capable of feeding and dressing themselves on
their own.

Patricia groaned once more for good measure before
bravely throwing off the covers. Immediately her body
was covered with goose bumps. Oh, to have the money
to adequately heat this old house!

Her feet hit the cold floorboards running. Experience
had taught her that the best cure for morning frigidity
was jumping under a hot shower just as fast as the tired,
old pipes would pump it. Bleary-eyed, she made her
way to the bathroom. The fact that light was leaking
out from around the bathroom door didn't necessarily
surprise her. Despite repeated warnings about wasting
energy, the boys often left the lights on after a midnight
foray to relieve themselves. She was mumbling something or other about money not growing on trees when
she stumbled into the bathroom. Cameron was just stepping out of the shower as she closed the door behind
her.

Patricia was too surprised to do anything but gape in
disbelief. She didn't even have the wherewithal to turn
around or even to blink as he snapped a towel off the
rack and wrapped it around himself with lightning
speed. Steam rose from his body in curling white ten-
drils. Water glistened in crystallite beads along his

broad shoulders and dripped in rivulets down the
smooth plane of his chest. She found Cameron's sleek,
muscular physique very much to her liking. The man
could have been sculpted out of marble by Michelan-
gelo. He was close enough to touch, and Patricia had
to fight the urge to run her fingertips over a map of thin,
jagged scars marring the surface of an otherwise perfect
body.

"You're early," was all she could manage to stammer.

Unable to decide whether her tone was apologetic or
accusatory, Cameron countered that blinding flash of
the obvious with a cockeyed smile to hide his own mor-
tification. "Or maybe you're right on time."

As if he wasn't already self-conscious enough about
standing half-naked at attention in front of the boss
lady, Cameron was doubly embarrassed to be doing so
in a bathroom that smelled so utterly feminine. Just because a fellow might be tempted to sniff at the heavenly
fragrances standing guard along the ledge of the tub
while he was under the shower, didn't make him the
kind of man who got into anything kinky, he hoped she
knew. Just one who couldn't resist this particular lady's
distinct scent. At the time it had not seemed particularly
untoward when he chose to use a dollop of her shampoo
to lather up his hair. Now all he could do was wonder
how in the world he was going to hide it from her when
the bottle was in plain sight with the cap off and *her*
light floral odor emanating from his skin.

Cameron felt her eyes follow the path of his blush
all the way from the base of his belly up to the roots
of his hair. He dropped his own gaze to encompass the
swell of her breasts against the thin cotton of her gown.
The flicker of desire in his eyes burst into a blue blaze

NO RISK, NO OBLIGATION TO BUY...NOW OR EVER!

GUARANTEED

PLAY "ROLL A DOUBLE" AND YOU GET FREE GIFTS! HERE'S HOW TO PLAY:

1. Peel off label from front cover. Place it in space provided at right. With a coin, carefully scratch off the silver dice. Then check the claim chart to see what we have for you – TWO FREE BOOKS and a mystery gift – ALL YOURS! ALL FREE!

2. Send back this card and you'll receive brand-new Silhouette Romance® novels. These books have a cover price of $3.50 each in the U.S. and $3.99 each in Canada, but they are yours to keep absolutely free.

3. There's no catch. You're under no obligation to buy anything. We charge nothing – ZERO – for your first shipment. And you don't have to make any minimum number of purchases – not even one!

4. The fact is, thousands of readers enjoy receiving books by mail from the Silhouette Reader Service™. They like the convenience of home delivery...they like getting the best new novels BEFORE they're available in stores...and they love our discount prices!

5. We hope that after receiving your free books you'll want to remain a subscriber. But the choice is yours – to continue or cancel any time at all! So why not take us up on our invitation, with no risk of any kind. You'll be glad you did!

The Silhouette Reader Service™ — Here's how it works:

Accepting your 2 free books and mystery gift places you under no obligation to buy anything. You may keep the books and gift and return the shipping statement marked "cancel." If you do not cancel, about a month later we'll send you 6 additional novels and bill you just $2.90 each in the U.S., or $3.25 each in Canada, plus 25¢ delivery per book and applicable taxes if any.* That's the complete price and — compared to the cover price of $3.50 in the U.S. and $3.99 in Canada — it's quite a bargain! You may cancel at any time, but if you choose to continue, every month we'll send you 6 more books, which you may either purchase at the discount price or return to us and cancel your subscription.

*Terms and prices subject to change without notice. Sales tax applicable in N.Y. Canadian residents will be charged applicable provincial taxes and GST.

If offer card is missing write to: Silhouette Reader Service, 3010 Walden Ave., P.O. Box 1867, Buffalo NY 14240-1867

BUSINESS REPLY MAIL
FIRST-CLASS MAIL   PERMIT NO. 717   BUFFALO, NY

POSTAGE WILL BE PAID BY ADDRESSEE

SILHOUETTE READER SERVICE
3010 WALDEN AVE
PO BOX 1867
BUFFALO NY 14240-9952

NO POSTAGE
NECESSARY
IF MAILED
IN THE
UNITED STATES

that threatened to consume them both. Seconds stretched between them. The look they shared was steamier than the heat fogging up the mirror. Through a haze of mist, they regarded each other as warily as two jungle cats.

"Mom!"

Patricia almost jumped out of her skin at the sound of Johnny pounding on the door. She frowned. The last thing she needed to do was explain to her ten-year-old how she and their foreman had ended up in the shower together.

She pulled the door open to face her son. A cloud of condensation enveloped the boy who had far more pressing things on his mind than his mother's obvious discomfort.

"I'm hungry," he said.

So am I, Cameron almost added with a feral look in his eyes. *But not for breakfast...*

Patricia grabbed her son's arm for support and guided Johnny toward the stairs. "Well, so much for my shower," she sighed.

"If you don't mind waiting outside a minute, I'll get changed and let you in. I'd be glad to rustle up breakfast for the crew."

That voice sounded a whole lot like his, but Cameron wasn't sure. Surely a fellow who couldn't so much as scramble an egg without burning it would not utter such an altruistic statement.

"You really wouldn't mind?" Patricia asked, her eyes widening in surprise.

"Not at all," Cameron lied. "That is, as long as cold cereal's good enough for you."

"It's what we always have," Johnny reassured him.

His mother refrained from cuffing him and shot him a look of censure. "Not always," she protested.

"No, not always," the boy quickly amended with an insincere lift of his eyebrows in Cameron's direction.

"And besides," Patricia interjected on an apologetic note, "the deal is I'm supposed to feed you, not the other way around."

"It would just be for one morning. You go on and take your shower and don't worry about a thing. I can handle it."

Had he lost his mind? He would just as soon try milking a Brahma bull as fix breakfast for a gaggle of hungry ragamuffins. His friends would have a hay day if they could see him wrangling big, old goofy birds and wearing an apron to boot. If the paparazzi got hold of such a damning snapshot, he could kiss any promotional contract goodbye forever.

"Thanks," Patricia said. "Thanks a lot."

A man could have gotten a toothache from the sweet, appreciative look she gave him.

"Think nothing of it. Take your time," he replied, making a sardonic mental note to make himself a dental appointment. Had it not been for the fact that he'd been so befuzzled in his state of undress at finding Patricia in the same room with him, Cameron was certain he would never have gone and trapped himself like this.

She stepped out in the hall and waited for him to get dressed. When he emerged moments later, an escort service was awaiting him. Johnny led Cameron down the hallway. As the bathroom door closed softly behind Patricia, he could hear the soothing sound of water running in the shower. It conjured up decadent images of a cotton nightgown abandoned upon the floor and a lithe body stepping gracefully over the lip of the tub. That dulcet sound was joined by the dubious harmony of a baby's wail. The discordance jarred him from pleasant illusions and plunged him into reality headfirst. What in the name of sanity had he let himself in for?

Patricia was hit full in the face with a blast of cold water. Hot water was at a premium, and Cameron had apparently used most of it up. On top of that, he had adjusted the showerhead so it fit *him* comfortably. Still, she wasn't complaining. The fact that the man had actually offered to lend a hand with breakfast was not to be taken lightly. Had her own husband been as helpful, she would have fallen over in shock. They all would have starved if Hadley had been in charge of feeding them.

She was less amused than disappointed to find the cap off her shampoo bottle. Her generic brand couldn't possibly compete with that masculine, slightly musky scent Cameron used. Even after a hard day of reshingling her roof, he smelled too good to be true. If a woman could bottle such a scent, Patricia figured she could make a fortune.

The temperature of the water may have been far from scalding, but Patricia's thoughts were not. That image of Cameron naked was a picture that would stay with her for life. Beneath a stream of tepid water, every detail of that gorgeous, masculine body came back into stark focus. She couldn't imagine how he had incurred such a multitude of scars. He looked rather like a beloved rag doll stitched and restitched against the wear and tear of time. The possibility such injuries might have been caused by a dangerous profession—like rodeo—hit her like a thundering herd of buffalo. Heavens to Betsy, could he possibly have been telling her the truth earlier?

More than likely he had won those injuries in barroom brawls, she decided, remembering that gigantic chip on his shoulder the day he arrived. Evel Knievel would have had second thoughts about jumping over it. The possibility that she may have misjudged the man was too disturbing to grant permanent easement to her conscious thought. Cameron's past would have to wait. All she needed to concern herself with right now was what was happening downstairs.

Finishing her shower in record time, Patricia hurried to brush her teeth. She did little more than rub a towel through her hair and apply a spot of lipstick before tossing on an old pair of jeans and an oversize flannel work shirt. Sticking out her tongue at her bedraggled image as she hurried past the mirror in the hallway, she reminded herself that there was no time for primping today—not when a stranger was alone in the kitchen with her three little angels.

The poor man!

Cameron was aghast to discover that there was barely enough packaged cereal left for Amy Leigh alone. Talk about kids eating one out of house and home! Just a few days ago he thought he'd bought enough groceries to feed a small army. Cameron set a bowl before the toddler and directed Amy to "eat up." She reacted with due deference by pelting him between the eyes with a handful of sticky puffed rice. Tossing a warning look over his shoulder, he abandoned her to a rainbow of colored marshmallow sprinkles.

Cereal crunched beneath his boots as he made his way to the refrigerator. There he was greeted by a couple of gigantic green emu eggs. Quickly he shut the door on them. He found a round container of oatmeal from the pantry and proceeded to read the directions, which looked simple enough for a ten-year-old to follow. He hoped Johnny wouldn't mind assisting him.

"Grab a pot," he instructed the boy, who immediately disappeared beneath the countertop.

Amid a clatter of metal, Johnny emerged a moment later wearing one on his head. "Guess who I am," he said, striking a pose.

"Johnny—"

"Appleseed," the lad supplied with a broad grin that faded the instant he saw Cameron pouring oatmeal into a measuring cup. "Ugggh," he offered in commentary.

Cameron's glare dared him to utter another desultory sound. The last thing he needed right now was a pint-size critic.

"Shouldn't your brother be up by now?" he asked, checking his watch.

"It takes a team of mules to drag him out of bed in the morning. Can we have cinnamon toast with that?"

"If you fix it yourself," Cameron replied, assuming the child could handle that simple task. "But go and get Kirk up first. Tell him *I* said it's past time for him to get up."

Though Johnny's sigh indicated his displeasure at being his brother's keeper, the dark look on Cameron's face stopped him from registering any complaints. Moments later angry sounds erupted from upstairs.

"Get up!"

"Get out of my room!"

"Get up!"

"Get out!"

These two lines formed alternating lyrics that persisted for at least a dozen refrains. When Cameron could not take it a second longer, he stomped over to the stairs and bellowed, "Do I need to come up there?"

As blessed silence broke out, he returned to the stove to find a gray mass boiling over the sides of the pot. In his haste to turn the burner off, he slipped on a trail of brightly colored cold cereal littering the floor.

Amy chortled in delight as she watched him do an interesting little step in hopes of maintaining his balance. Cameron came down on his backside hard enough to knock the open box of oatmeal to the floor.

"Son of a—"

Three innocent faces peered down at him.

"—gun!" Cameron spat out with all the intended vehemence of the word he generally preferred when he went buns up.

Somehow the boys managed to get more cinnamon and sugar on the floor than on their toast, but they dutifully took their places before two heaping bowls of oatmeal. Sticking a spoon in his, Johnny offered an opinion.

"It looks just like the Awful Tower," he said of the angle and position of his spoon suspended in the gluey substance.

A smile threatened to crack the grim mask Cameron wore. Apparently the little guy had been studying "hysteric" landmarks in school.

"Don't you mean Eiffel?"

"I guess. My teacher says if I don't learn how to say the words right, I'll end up like Rudolf the Reindeer."

Cameron knew better than to ask, but he couldn't resist nevertheless. "And how's that?"

"I'll go down in history."

The boy laughed so hard at his own joke that Cameron was unable to refrain from joining in.

"Speaking of history, it looks to me like Sherman marched right through my kitchen."

Patricia stepped into the room and looked around in bewilderment. Sugar, oatmeal, cinnamon and cold cereal covered the floor in a fascinating collage of colors and textures. The smell of burned oatmeal lingered in the air, and it looked like a volcano had erupted on top of her stove.

Cameron met her gaze sheepishly.

She took a step toward him.

Crunch!

"I can not believe—"

She took another step. *Crunch!*

"—that you actually—"

Step. *Crunch!*

"—actually suffered through all this without calling for help."

Crunch! Crunch!

Cameron's mouth fell open in amazement as she stopped in front of him and produced a wobbly smile. Bonnie had been a dervish in the kitchen, always scolding him for leaving the tiniest mess behind, and he was prepared for anything. Rage, remonstrance, feminine tears... Anything but an outpouring of gratitude.

"I'm sorry about all this, but—"

Patricia interrupted him by placing a feather-soft kiss upon his cheek. "Don't even think of apologizing for the sweetest gesture any man has ever done for me."

She had to be kidding! What kind of personal hell had this lady endured to be so touched by such a simple thing as having a little "help" in the kitchen?

Kirk pointed at him and giggled. "You've got lipstick on your cheek."

Johnny snickered behind the safety of his napkin.

Cameron ran his thumb over the stain of *Come Hither Pink* warpaint upon his face and blushed furiously. Like some stupid schoolboy, he thought to himself. Like some shy virgin, for Pete's sake.

The brush of Patricia's lips upon his skin left him feeling tingly all over. Her hair glistening with water, the woman looked and smelled like a bouquet of fresh-picked flowers, and he had the wild desire to sweep her into his arms and give her a sampling of what a real kiss was all about.

Cameron looked at her.

Patricia looked at him.

Seconds ticked by, and the moment slipped away as softly as a butterfly flitting through a field of blossoms. Patricia grabbed a broom and started cleaning up. She spoke to the children without looking up from her task.

"Cameron worked real hard to fix you that breakfast. You boys go on and eat it."

Ignoring the looks of disgust pasted on their faces, she turned her attention to filling the sink with hot, soapy water. It was her guess that a week of soaking wouldn't be near enough to dislodge that baked-on blackened gunk on her favorite pot. She picked it up by the handle and submerged it.

"Here, let me help," Cameron offered, taking the pot from her. That familiar electrical current zinged between them again as his hand grazed hers. Sparks flew in all directions. Surely there was no more dangerous combination than electricity and water. A zillion volts rooted them both to the spot.

"There's no need," Patricia assured him. "Just as soon as I get the children off to school, I'll fix you something more—" she searched for the right word "—filling."

Cameron smiled at the delicious thought of skipping breakfast altogether and nibbling instead on something a little spicier in the absence of prying eyes. "Don't you mean fix breakfast for *us*?" he asked, his voice soft and inviting. "I don't believe you've eaten yet, either."

"Can't. I've got to tend to the stock."

Stock. There was that appalling misnomer again. He gritted his teeth against it and watched his sexual fantasies disappear before the mundane obligations of the day.

"Those idiotic birds are hardly more important than your health."

Patricia took Cameron's irritability in stride. He looked more disheveled this morning than she'd ever seen him before. Taking care of a houseful of kids was far more taxing than most men realized. She'd wager even crawling back up on the roof again was preferable to being subjected to any more torment at the hands of the Hellion Three.

"What exactly have you got against emus?" she asked, taking him to task for the affront to her birds. Quite the opposite of what he thought, they really were very intelligent creatures. She wished he would at least take the time to understand them and their habits.

"They're ugly, they stink, and they keep me awake all night with their strange caterwauling."

Patricia felt a telltale tremor in her tummy. An entirely different bird was keeping her awake at night. One with a sexy mustache and eyes as blue as a clear mountain lake. "Tell me," she said, falling headlong into the depths of that very lake, "is there anything you like less than emus?"

Cameron answered with a single, well-considered word.

"Children."

There. He had drawn a line in the sand that he was certain Patricia would never step over.

She met his measuring look with one of her own and tossed in a lopsided grin.

"Just who are you trying to convince, Cameron? Me? Or yourself?"

Chapter Eight

For a man who claimed to dislike children, Cameron sure was good with them. Patricia had a theory about children and animals having an innate sense about who to trust, and whether her foreman wanted to admit it or not, he was a gigantic magnet for kids and critters alike.

Seeing how Patricia's own offspring didn't exactly take to just anybody, that was saying a lot. Since their father's death, the children seemed intent on scaring off any potential suitors. Not that there had been all that many. Just the veterinarian, Jim Guptill, who came out once to take a look at a sick emu, and Elliott Coleman who still lived with his own mother and blushed three shades of purple the one time he had screwed up enough courage to ask her to lunch at the local drive-in. All of her children, the baby included, reacted to anyone who showed the slightest interest in their mother, with a protective petulance that fell just short of outright rudeness. Why, the last time she'd run into Jim at the grocery store, the kids had behaved so badly, pulling on her sleeve and whining to go, all the while furtively loading all sorts of expensive contraband into her cart, that Patricia almost had a heart attack when the girl rang up her total at the checkout stand.

She had, of course, refused Jim's magnanimous offer to pay for her groceries but thought it extremely generous of him to even suggest it. It was at such times that Patricia couldn't help wondering what it would be like to have the support of a man with a steady, respectable job and the desire to provide for her.

"I don't like him," Johnny had said in no uncertain terms. "He's got weasel eyes."

Kirk slanted his own eyes at her and poured on the guilt. "I don't think Daddy would have liked him, either."

It rankled Patricia that her children reacted to other men's solicitousness with such contempt only to turn right around and embrace Cameron's cantankerousness with open arms. Even the emus that he so openly loathed could not seem to resist the man's dubious charm.

Patricia found it hysterical how they took to him. Every time he walked past the corral, the birds lined up like a gaggle of teenage girls watching the local football hero go by. On those occasions when he had to actually step inside their pens, they flocked around him and regaled the heavens with the sound of their high-pitched squeals. Cameron generally reacted by kicking at them and mumbling something unintelligible under his breath.

When Patricia ventured the opinion that they might be attracted to his particular scent, he skewered her with a look that would have put a lesser woman in the hospital.

"Surely you aren't suggesting it's my cologne that's making them attack me?" he asked in disbelief at the very thought. "They just like provoking me."

Rubbing her chin, Patricia feigned deep thought. "It's just a simple matter of attraction. I wouldn't fight it if I were you."

Cameron responded in a voice loaded with gravel. "I wouldn't fight it, either—if it weren't some tom-fool birds you were talking about but a hot little chick instead."

Patricia's heart skipped a beat. Then another.

Was he actually flirting with her?

Just because his eyes had darkened with innuendo didn't necessarily mean he was referring to her. It had been so long since she'd played that age-old game that she'd almost forgotten the rules. She could hardly admit that his scent drove her crazy, too. The way it lingered in her towels after his morning showers was especially nice, so much so in fact that she found herself surreptitiously stealing a secret moment to inhale deeply before depositing it onto her daily laundry pile.

Instead she faked a nonchalance she did not feel and asked, "You really like ruffling feathers, don't you? Be it fowl or fair…"

Cameron blinked in disbelief.

Had she actually winked at him?

More than likely she was just trying to get something out of her eye. Like that unladylike gleam that sent a surge of passion raging through his body.

Squaring off beneath the fading heat of the late-afternoon sun, they acknowledged the push-pull of their mutual attraction. And for an instant both allowed themselves to succumb to it, both imagining what it might be like to enter into a relationship unfettered by old baggage, ulterior motives, opposing personalities. And children.

Children!

"Oh, shoot!" Patricia said with a start. "I've got to pick up the kids at the bus stop."

Good Lord, she'd been so caught up in an inadvisable flirtation with the hired man that she'd almost forgotten her own children! What kind of a mother was she, anyway? One she'd wager Cameron would peg a complete coward by the swiftness of her departure.

When she returned a short time later, Patricia was certain she had her hormones and her thoughts under control. Unfortunately, the instant her boys burst out of the truck and hurled themselves at Cameron like human cannonballs, her heart went all soft and mushy again.

"Don't bother Mr. Wade, boys," she hollered after them.

"He doesn't mind," Johnny tossed back over his shoulder. "Do you, Cameron?"

"Not much," he grumbled under his breath. It was awfully hard to refuse children who were so grateful for the smallest kindness shown them.

Amy pulled away from her mother. "Me go, too," she gurgled.

Patricia grabbed for her, but the girl was amazingly fast for her little legs. Giggling at the game she had made, Amy dodged her mother as she chased her around the yard.

"It's like trying to run down a superball," Patricia gasped.

In light of the girl's determination, Cameron capitulated. "That's all right. She can come, too." He narrowed his eyes at the boys. "Her brothers'll look after her."

They knew better than to argue. Once again Patricia was struck by the respect the boys paid this man. Had Cameron actually pandered to their obvious hero worship, they could not have been more deferential. The man had been here less than a week, and already a pattern was emerging. If they stayed out from under his feet and did as they were told, Cameron allowed them to tag along and idolize every step he took.

It had only taken him a few days to finish the roof, and he'd already started in on a number of other odd jobs around the place without waiting for Patricia to point them out. For a woman used to doing everything on her own, she wasn't so sure she liked him acting so completely independently of her, almost as if he owned the place. A shiver of foreboding rippled through her as she watched the painstaking measures he took to show the children the technique used to replace the broken window that Hadley had boarded over with plywood the very day he had been killed. She hoped the children didn't somehow get the idea that their father could be replaced as easily as that pane of glass.

That night after dinner, she was even more aware of Cameron's masculine presence than usual. Johnny sought his advice on his math homework. As Patricia finished the dishes, she noticed her oldest voiced none of his usual objections to Cameron's insistence that he not only show all of his work but also to do so in a legible manner. Rather than argue about how stupid the assignment was, Johnny settled right down and completed his work in record time. Afterward Kirk dragged out a well-worn Dr. Seuss book and asked Cameron to read him a bedtime story. Not two months ago, he had avowed to his mother that he was too old for such "baby stuff" and was even beginning to chafe at the thought of being tucked in at night.

If a story was going to be read, Amy wanted to be in on it. Tucking her favorite kitty into a doll buggy, she extended Cameron her chubby little arms in hopes of being picked up herself.

"Sorry, kid," Cameron grumbled. "I'm not about to have 'you know what' running all down my shirt."

Amy stuck out her lower lip and regarded him with silent reproval. Meanwhile Mittens took advantage of the opportunity to make a break for freedom and scampered out of the room before the child could get her in another headlock.

Patricia immediately set down her dishrag and attempted to comfort her little fusspot. "There, there sweetheart," she said, sweeping the toddler into her arms.

The look the girl gave Cameron over her mother's shoulder was so reproachful it caused him to mutter something about the fury of a woman scorned.

"All right, everybody," Patricia announced. "I want you to leave Cameron alone. He's been a real good sport, but now it's time for bed."

Johnny and Kirk simultaneously rallied forces.

"Aww, Mom!"

Cameron silenced their protests with a single warning glance. They obediently trudged up the stairs without another peep.

He was grateful to Patricia for saving him from the attack her children were waging on his heart. Emotional entanglement with this brood was not a risk Cameron was willing to take. Just being back in the presence of such a tight-knit family brought back too many painful memories. Memories of a mother who had died so poor two years after his father had lost this place that they had to take out a loan to pay for the funeral. Cameron had been in junior high when he buried his mother and witnessed his father lay his heart to rest beside her. John Wade never recovered from the loss, and Cameron learned a lesson that had stuck with him for life. Love equals pain.

The one time he had forgotten that, Bonnie had driven the point home again with one hand wrapped around the knife in his back and the other in his billfold.

"Tuck me in?" Amy implored, puckering her little Kewpie-doll lips at him.

Cameron stared at the child in bewilderment. How could one tell a mere baby that love is for suckers? That he was more afraid of her beguiling innocence than of all the big bad bulls he'd ever encountered?

"Amy doll!" her mother scolded. "Quit pestering the poor man. I'll tuck you in like always."

Cameron knew what she really meant was *That's my job! Not one for strangers who don't even belong in our midst...*

Why did that hurt him so? After all, he had made it perfectly clear he didn't even want to pick the child up. Nobody but him needed to know that he was afraid of breaking the pretty little thing.

Flinching from the imagined reproach in Patricia's voice, he retaliated with deliberate antagonism. While love was definitely out of the picture, he didn't mind letting Patricia know he wasn't at all opposed to sex in and of itself.

"You're welcome to tuck me in when you're done with the kids."

Her reaction was not what he expected at all. Rather

than being slapped by an open palm for such cheekiness, Cameron felt the sting of her laughter instead.

"I didn't realize you thought of me as your mommy."

At the affront, Cameron boiled over in frustration. "Oh, honey, let me assure you I don't think of you as my mother."

As smooth as whisky, his voice was sweetened by the sudden endearment. Patricia struggled through a heart-stopping moment of self-revelation before admitting with a shrug, "Then maybe the problem is that I find you a little too much like my father."

Cameron could tell by the tight lines edging her mouth that he was not being complimented. He wondered what kind of parent had put such lingering sorrow into those beautiful, haunted eyes? He fought the urge to reach out and smooth away the furrows in her forehead, to cup her chin in his hands, to kiss away her doubts, to chase away her ghosts.

They were grown people for heaven's sake. A sexual dalliance didn't have to mean a plunge into their respective pasts. Did it?

Only if it was to mean something…

It was a chance Cameron wasn't willing to take. He didn't have to remind himself how unfair that would be to a woman like Patricia, a single mother in a conservative community trying to do her best by her children. He'd do well to remember that his primary intention was not to bed the woman but to rip her home out from under her. Cameron swallowed against the hard ball forming in his throat. It had been a whole lot easier to feel virtuous about his well-laid plans before he'd actually ever met Patricia.

And before he'd begun to be sucked in by those mischievous, big-eyed kids of hers.

Chapter Nine

After so many years of yearning for some masculine help around the place, Patricia couldn't understand why she was suddenly so resentful of all the little things Cameron was doing to make her life easier.

Most women would gush with appreciation, but she was not most women. Having lived eighteen years with a domineering father who ruled his household with an iron fist, she had deliberately sought out someone his complete opposite for a partner in marriage. Whereas her father was a control freak, her husband had been more than happy to let Patricia run things however she saw fit. And as much as she had sometimes become annoyed with his lackadaisical attitude, Patricia had only to remember her mother kowtowing night and day to her father to feel grateful for Hadley's easygoing nature. It certainly made for a more enjoyable childhood for her offspring than the one she remembered.

She would never forget the time that she had returned from her first date at the ripe age of sixteen to find her room ransacked. Roland D'Winter had claimed it was his parental duty to root out any signs of dangerous teenage rebellion, but Patricia had felt deeply violated by his lack of trust. She knew it had more to do with his reaction to her budding sexuality than with anything she had ever done to warrant his suspicion. The instant she was graduated from high school, Patricia had eloped with Hadley, vowing along with her fidelity to never lose her identity in marriage like her mother had.

Considering her resistance to her own father's authority, it struck her odd that her children were so drawn to Cameron Wade's commanding presence. While she understood that their affection for the man was tied to their need for a strong male role model, Patricia herself found accepting his help rather like swallowing an aspirin without water. The fact that it was good for her didn't make it go down any easier.

She had no desire to become reliant on any man— especially one guaranteed to be miles down the road the instant the terms of his contract were fulfilled. Three months might not be enough time for Cameron to accomplish miracles around the place, but it certainly offered ample opportunity for her children to be irreparably hurt when their hero hit the road without thought to what he was leaving behind in his aftermath.

Considering that fact, Patricia decided it would be best for everyone concerned to limit her foreman's duties to work outside the house. It was hardly fair to expect more of him. The running of her household and raising of her children were to remain completely her domain. And if that meant she was tired and out of sorts at times, then so be it. She was not about to relinquish control of her family to some drifter whose eyes glittered with promises he had no intention of honoring.

* * *

Cameron tucked himself into bed blaming the painful bout of nostalgia that hit him with such force earlier in the evening upon that silly old Dr. Seuss book. It had been one of his favorites as a child. The mere sight of it evoked memories of his mother holding him on her lap and reading to him. It grieved him to realize that such golden moments could never be regained—unless, of course, a man was fortunate enough to be allowed to repeat them with children of his own.

It was the most startling thought Cameron Wade had ever entertained in his entire life. One he was certain would have never entered his mind before this special family had begun to work their sorcery upon him.

He hardened himself against it, remembering the way Patricia had recoiled from her children's attempts to include him in their nighttime rituals. After she'd made such a point to let him know what a bad influence she considered him, he'd be darned if he'd let her see how much it would have meant to him to read her kids a stupid bedtime story. He had noticed how she'd bristled when Johnny had asked for him to help with his homework. Cameron suspected she would be up half the night rechecking his work. That she might think him too dumb for fourth grade math blistered his ego.

He told himself that he didn't care. If the fool woman was so determined to get along without any help from him, why should he bother trying to change her mind? It had been his experience that logic didn't stand a chance against raging hormones and female stubbornness.

On the roof or in the kitchen, Patricia Erhart seemed eminently capable of fending for her family all by herself. That she was too proud for her own good was none of his business. Cameron told himself he would do well to remember that he was neither husband nor father around here, but merely a hired hand. And as nice as being included in the circle of this family's love would be, it was in his best interests never to forget that despite being born and raised here, he was for all intents and purposes an outsider. He had been since the day his family had relinquished their control over this land and would be until the day he formally reclaimed it. Until that happened, he suspected there would always be a little boy trapped inside him. A little boy with his nose pressed against the window of his own home. Begging to get back in.

The lonesome sound of coyotes baying at the moon set the emus outside his window to squawking in distress. Cameron wished the coyotes would hurry up and make a finger-licking feast of feathers and flesh before the morning light. Unfortunately, he suspected the predators were far too wily to be lured so close to danger for such a measly mouthful of fluff. He pulled his pillow over his head. What with all the racket going on, he doubted whether he'd be able to get a minute's honest sleep. Maybe if he were lucky, the sound would drown out that dull ache in his heart.

He didn't have to look far for an excuse to stay as removed from the house as possible. The following morning at the breakfast table, Patricia assessed him through bleary eyes.

"Have you ever been exposed to chicken pox?" she asked.

"My brother and I had 'em at the same time when we were kids. Why?"

"Because sometime between two and three this morning Amy came down with them."

No wonder she looked so completely exhausted. Cameron figured that Patricia must have been awakened by her daughter's cries just about the time he was finally drifting off to sleep.

"Luckily," she continued over a yawn, "the boys both were exposed when they were babies."

Despite his resolve to remain detached from this lady's plight, sympathy tugged at Cameron's heartstrings. She looked beat. Still remembering the disaster that had been made of the kitchen the last time he'd volunteered his assistance in the kitchen, he was reluctant to offer his services.

"Anything I can do to help out?"

"No."

It hadn't been a full eight hours since she'd vowed not to let this man undermine her confidence in her ability to take care of things on her own. But the thought of having to awaken Amy after she'd just now gotten her back to sleep was almost more than she could bear.

"That is, unless you wouldn't mind taking the boys to the bus stop for me?" she added weakly.

"I'd rather do that than be stuck here with a sick baby certain to wake up the instant her mother pulls out of the driveway," he replied honestly. An image of a child covered in red blisters bawling her head off for the better part of a half hour made him long for the relative tranquility of bull riding.

"All right!" Kirk beamed, obviously delighted with the thought of spending more time with Cameron. Over a bowl of cold cereal, he shared a smile with an older brother who did nothing to hide his own enthusiasm with these arrangements.

"I'd appreciate it," Patricia said.

Cameron wondered if she would choke on the words.

"I'll try my best not to be too bad an influence on them while you're not there to oversee my role modeling."

A night of tossing and turning beneath a heavy conscience and a heightened libido hadn't done much for his disposition, either.

Patricia opened her mouth to respond with an appropriate snappy comeback, but the sound of her daughter crying out in the next room replaced it with a worn-out sigh.

The slump of her shoulders as she headed for the stairs made Cameron regret the harsh tone of his words.

"Come on, boys," he prompted. "Your mother's had a rough night. Let's clean up the kitchen for her and get out of her hair just as quick as we can."

By the time Patricia got the baby calmed down, the dishes were done and the boys were on their way to school. There was just enough time for her to sneak in either a shower or a catnap before Cameron returned. Though one look in the mirror told her that both were needed, Amy nonetheless refused to allow her mother out of her sight for a single second. Scratching at the blotches on her face only made them itch worse, and Patricia's attempt to protect her by putting socks over her hands infuriated the tot beyond all reasoning.

"Hush," Patricia implored.

She grabbed a tattered medical volume off the shelf and perused the section on chicken pox while trying to soothe the toddler in her arms with a gentle rocking motion. The book did little more than remind her of the hell her next couple of days was going to be.

Recommended treatment included lots of rest, liquid, and patience on the part of the caretaker. Unfortunately, although Amy was burning up, getting liquids down her was like trying to put out a forest fire with a squirt gun. The girl resisted any attempt to be put to bed and fought like an angry cub when her mother tried slathering her with lotion.

Patricia managed little more than to run a brush through her own hair before Cameron returned from dropping the boys off at the bus stop. Looking and feeling the way she did, she was glad when he went straight to work without stopping at the house first.

As much as she hated depending on anyone else, Patricia was grateful to him. His offer to take care of the boys this morning had truly been a godsend, and the amount of work the man produced was nothing short of amazing. The roof was as good as new, the storm windows were up and ready for the first blast of Wyoming winter winds, the deepest, most dangerous ruts in the driveway had been filled in, and he'd begun repairs on the front porch with an almost reverential attitude.

When he failed to stop for lunch, Patricia assumed he either didn't want to bother her when she was tending to a sick child or he was still mad that she had expressed her concerns about his influence upon the boys. She was too tired to spend much time pondering it. Wrapping his sandwich in cellophane, she hoped he wouldn't mind having it for dinner.

Her head was ringing with Amy's incessant crying and lack of sleep. Her nerves were shot. She'd accomplished little more all day than keeping the girl from scratching herself into a bloody pulp and maintaining a tenuous grasp on her own sanity. On top of everything else, a sharp little tooth was trying to pop through Amy's tender gums.

At around three o'clock in the afternoon, Cameron opened the front door and hollered, "I'm going to pick up the boys from school now."

Patricia dragged herself to the entryway. She hadn't asked him to assume her duties as chauffeur and couldn't quite believe he'd remembered the appointed time on his own. A Post-it note stuck to Hadley's forehead couldn't have accomplished as much.

"Thank you," she said. "You don't have to be afraid to come in, you know. We're not exactly quarantined here."

"I know," Cameron said, but he took a step backward nonetheless.

Feeling like a leper, Patricia ran a tired hand through her hair.

"How about if I run on into town and pick up a pizza so you don't have to cook tonight," he suggested.

Had she not already had a stew simmering in the Crock-Pot, Patricia would have taken him up on the thoughtful offer. In between bouts of Amy's wailing she had managed to chop up enough vegetables to cover the soup bones at the bottom of the pot. It might not have been much, but it stood as a fragrant reminder that she was still capable of managing on her own.

"Thank you, but I have everything under control."

Feeling as useless as a crumb beneath her feet, Cameron wondered how long it would take her to sweep him away like Bonnie had. His gaze hardened. "Of course you do," he drawled.

Was he making fun of her? Patricia took a swipe at the dark circles beneath her eyes. The tips of her fingers felt as rough as the timbre in Cameron's voice. As rough as the sound of gravel crunching beneath the heels of his cowboy boots as he turned his back on her and strode off without another word.

Patricia appreciated the fact that Cameron kept the boys occupied and out from under her feet right up until dinnertime. Thick and hearty, the stew stood alone except for a hunk of cheese served on the side. Cameron ate every drop and even polished off the dried-out sandwich he'd missed at lunch without complaint. Cranky and teething, Amy refused to eat anything but Popsicles.

"Stew again?" Kirk asked, making a face at the enormous amount of vegetables dominating his bowl.

"Mind your manners," Cameron warned.

"How come she doesn't have to eat stew?" the boy whined, nodding in his sister's direction.

Grape Popsicle juice running down her chin in purple rivulets, Amy pounded on her high chair like it was a drum.

"Uh, Mom?" Johnny interjected sheepishly. "Did I forget to tell you I need some cupcakes for the class bake sale tomorrow?"

Patricia rested her head against the palms of both hands and counted to ten to keep from screaming.

As deep as the rumble of a big engine, Cameron's voice soothed her jangled nerves. "If you boys'll finish up all your food, I just might be persuaded to take you into town for ice cream cones at the Dairy Barn. I bet we could even pick up a dozen cupcakes at the bakery while we're in town."

Although not above bribery herself on occasion, Patricia glowered in his direction. Was it so completely obvious that she was coming apart at the seams? She wished she had the energy to show him by whipping up a delicious batch of homemade goodies for her son's class. Wished her pride didn't stick in her craw so. Wished Cameron had asked her to come along for ice cream, too. Wished she could better resist his reckless, thoughtful charm.

As if reading her mind, Cameron turned his attention from the children to her. "How about it, Patricia? Do you want to come along, or would you rather have some peace and quiet instead?"

"I'd better keep Amy inside."

Patricia was embarrassed to hear the disappointment registering in her voice. How low had she sunk when a simple outing to the Dairy Barn sounded like an exotic excursion?

"I wouldn't want to expose anybody else's children to chicken pox."

"Makes sense," Cameron responded easily.

Far more sense than the way his eyes glittered with sensual fire. Patricia wondered if she was becoming delirious. What man could look at such a disheveled and tired woman the way Cameron was looking at her? As though ice cream was the absolute last thing on his mind.

"I'm ready!" announced Johnny, sweeping his empty bowl off the table and heading for the sink.

"Me, too," chimed in Kirk as he raced his brother to the sink.

"I'll be back soon," Cameron assured her with a conspiratorial wink.

Patricia blanched at the promise. She squeezed her eyes shut as the ground beneath her feet tilted back and forth like some crazy carnival ride. He couldn't have known that those were the last words Hadley had ever said to her.

Cameron reached out to steady her and found her skin hot to the touch. Silken fire beneath his fingertips.

"Why, you're burning up!" he exclaimed, his eyes widening in surprise.

She swayed, fighting the impulse to rest her aching head against that rock-solid shoulder if only for a fraction of a second.

Don't go! she longed to say.

The boys fidgeted impatiently. Johnny shifted his weight from one foot to the other.

"Maybe I should stay," Cameron ventured. The look of concern on his face appeared genuine.

"Go on, and have fun," she croaked. "You don't want to disappoint the boys."

Go on before you discover the real reason I'm on fire. Before you discover the power you have over me. Before I have to admit to myself the feelings I have for a man who's so utterly wrong for me.

"Are you sick?" he persisted.

"I can't be. It's a rule, you know. Mommies aren't allowed to get sick." Patricia's smile was as off center as her humor.

Clamoring to be free, Amy threw a Popsicle stick across the room. "Down!" she demanded, and repeated herself a half dozen more times just to make sure she got her point across.

Kirk tugged on Cameron's sleeve. "We could bring you back a milk shake," he suggested.

"Chocolate please."

As Johnny grabbed Cameron's other sleeve, Patricia turned away to fumble with the belt that fastened her daughter to her high chair. She hoped Cameron didn't notice that her hands were shaking.

"Have fun," she said while doing her best to disguise the shiver of dread in her voice. "And drive carefully. There's a lot of wildlife on the road this time of night."

Patricia awoke slowly as if feeling her way through a heavy fog. It took her a moment to figure out just where she was. When her eyes adjusted to the darkness, she realized she was in the living room where she had fallen asleep on the couch with Amy nestled in a ball beneath her chin. Somebody kind had draped a blanket over the two of them before heading off to bed himself. Patricia shifted and tried getting to her feet without awakening the baby. She checked her watch. They had been asleep for almost four solid hours. The longest either had managed in the past twenty-four.

A light had been left on in the kitchen, and for once Patricia was grateful for the boys' lack of concern for the electric bill. She made her way up the stairs by the light. As she laid Amy down, the tot stuck her thumb into her mouth, adjusting to the change in surroundings with a loud, comfortable suck. Patricia wound the music box, sewn into a favored blue teddy bear, before flicking on the nightlight and tiptoeing out of the room. She took a moment to check on the boys and found both neatly tucked into their respective beds.

Her stomach grumbled, reminding her of the supper she had neglected to eat. She headed back to the kitchen for a snack and was in the process of opening the refrigerator door when a fluttering paper caught her eye. Affixed to the door with a magnet was the math assignment Cameron had helped Johnny complete. The teacher had underlined the red letter *A* twice and added a scratch 'n' sniff "Good Work" sticker as an extra motivational measure.

Patricia opened the refrigerator door with a telltale tremor to her hand. A chilly blast of air rushed out at her. The mist blurring her eyesight confused her. She had stood the pain of great loss with the stoicism of a Spartan, not so much as shedding a tear at her husband's funeral. Why the sight of a chocolate malt melting in her refrigerator would make her burst into tears was completely beyond her understanding.

Chapter Ten

Chapter Ten

Breakfast was a mumble of strained courtesies. With the exception of that blessed stretch of sleep on the couch, courtesy of Cameron's Caretaking Service, the rest of Patricia's night had been nightmarish. Amy had awakened every hour on the hour, tearful, itching and indignant. Nothing Patricia did budged either her temperature or her disposition. Between the teething and the pox, Patricia was at wit's end.

She suspected she was sick herself. Sick with worry about Amy's health. About whether she was doing an adequate job raising her children. About whether she would be able to pay the bills for another month. Whether she had made the right choice to stay in Wyoming and not succumb to her father's demands that they go "home." But most of all she was worried about whether she was falling in love.

The fact that Cameron showed up at the table bearing a huge box of doughnuts did little to put her mind at ease. It was going to be darned hard not to miss such

kind favors when the man got his fill of Ranch Pande-
monium and struck out for the horizon, sighing in relief.
Glancing at the calendar hanging on the wall, Patricia
counted off the remaining length of his contract. Time
was rapidly slipping by.

Reading the fatigue in Patricia's expression, Cameron
ordered the boys to gather up a handful of doughnuts
to eat on the road. They wolfed them down on the way
out the door.

"Bye, Mom," they mumbled through mouthfuls.
"See ya after school."

There was concern in his gaze as Cameron ordered,
"You take it easy, now."

His eyes refused to release her gaze until she nodded
in agreement. The protective warning, glittering in those
blue depths, sent a thrumming feminine awareness rushing through her. She averted her eyes as demurely as a
schoolgirl.

"I mean it," he reiterated. "Just as soon as the boys
are safely on their way to school, I'll be back to help."

They weren't out of the driveway before Patricia was
at the medicine cabinet searching for relief. She thought
her head was going to explode. The throbbing was so
painful it felt like a chorus line was tap dancing on her
temples. She shook a couple of aspirin out of a bottle
and forced them down in one big gulp.

The baby wasn't hungry for anything put in front of
her. Not for oatmeal, for puréed fruits, even for that
good old standby—Popsicles. Each entree landed on the
floor with an accompanying shriek of disapproval.

Patricia found herself at that point between sleep-
lessness and irritability where parents can so easily be
pushed over the edge. A shrill voice bubbled out of
some pocket of frustration deep inside her that she

didn't recognize as her own. Surely that incoherent babble belonged to a monster. She suspected if she were to glance in a mirror, Frankenmommy would be staring back at her.

Big things like the repeated loss of their investments and her husband's death she handled amazingly well. It was the little things like the baby's incessant crying, a mounting pile of debt and the uncertainty in her own heart about her feelings for a man she did not completely trust that threatened to overpower her.

Patricia moaned. Covering her face with her hands, she crumpled into a ball against the sink and tried to block out a world that was crushing the life out of her.

Cameron could not believe his eyes when he returned to the ranch a short time later. Seemingly unattended, Amy sat in the middle of a floor littered with an interesting collection of pots and pans. At the realization that her mother was nowhere in sight, a surge of panic set Cameron's heart ringing like the clapper in a warning bell.

"Hey there, little darlin'!" he murmured, stooping to pick Amy up.

She wrapped her sticky arms around the strong column of his neck and sniffled into the open collar of his shirt. Though it tickled, Cameron was in no mood for laughing. He wouldn't be until he located the girl's mother and put his mind at rest.

Stepping around the kitchen counter, he made his way to the sink and was stopped in his tracks at the sight of Patricia huddled against the sideboard. She reminded him of a seashell, curled protectively upon herself.

"Are you all right?"

She didn't so much as look up. It seemed to take a Herculean effort for her to simply nod her head and acknowledge his presence.

Cameron turned the faucet on and ran some warm water over a washcloth. He wiped Amy's face off and set her down. Immediately she began wailing. Remembering that it had worked before, he pulled his grandpa's gold watch out of his pocket and handed it to her. She grinned up at him before toddling off into the living room teething on her new "toy." Neither the sentimental or actual value of the antique was of any concern to Cameron at the moment. The sight of Patricia curled in a fetal position sent a shaft of fear coursing through every nerve in his body.

He squatted beside her and softly asked, "What's the matter, darlin'?"

There it was again. That same mellifluous endearment that he employed in the comforting of crybabies of all ages.

"Nothing!" Patricia insisted, choking back her tears. The chances of him sticking around after witnessing such a psychotic episode were astronomically small.

Draping an arm around her shoulders, Cameron drew her close to him. His sinewy strength was both solid and gentle. Clean, he smelled of masculine cologne. Of woods and wind and wildness restrained.

"Nothing?" he persisted, brushing the hair away from her face. Fascinated by the way it caught the light streaming through the window, he lingered a moment over its silky texture. Reminded of a frightened animal caught in a trap, he petted her and softly repeated her name.

"Everything..." The word came out half whisper, half sob.

"It can't be as bad as all that." Cameron's drawl was as sweet and sticky as sun-warmed honey. "Why don't you let me take a turn with Amy? Take a little nap or better yet a nice long walk."

"You'd do that for me?" Patricia sniffled in disbelief.

"Why wouldn't I?"

Once again Cameron found himself wondering what kind of man Patricia's husband had been. Piecing together her own reactions and some of the things the children had said, he was inclined to believe the lout had never so much as lifted a finger to help out. Yet Patricia seemed determined to protect his memory with religious fervor. Secretly Cameron dubbed Hadley St. DoLittle the Spineless, patron of good times and irresponsibility. He supposed that covering for her husband's flaws had helped make Patricia such a strong individual.

It was a shock to discover that behind that Super Woman mask she donned each day was a vulnerable little girl fighting to prove she was able to have it all and do it all by herself—without the assistance of some clumsy man underfoot. Now that her invisible mask was smashed and scattered into a thousand pieces at her feet, Cameron felt a fierce possessiveness well up inside of himself. Never before had he felt such a strong urge to make a woman his own and safeguard her against the world. The intensity of that feeling hit him like a ton of wet sand.

Taking her hand into his, Cameron stood up and pulled Patricia to her feet. The tingle of his touch radiated from her fingertips to all her limbs, settling at last in the pit of her stomach where it lingered in sweet, undulating waves.

"Don't you worry about a thing, darlin'. We'll get along just fine. You've just been cooped up too long in this house, working way too hard without enough sleep. You just need to take a little time for yourself, that's all. God knows you deserve it. Go on and take your walk."

Her eyes looked blank, but she nodded mutely.

"And don't come back until you're good and ready."

Patricia was afraid that once she started walking she would never come back. Just walking away from it all seemed the most sensible solution at the moment, and visions of hitching a ride out of town danced in her mind. But to her surprise the most amazing thing happened while she was ambling along. Ten short minutes ago she was going out of her head, in angst over life being nothing more than one disparaging moment strung to the next when suddenly she noticed how incredibly blue the sky was. She stopped walking for a minute and allowed herself to be completely transfixed by the beauty of the color. It matched a certain pair of eyes that had been haunting her dreams.

In the absence of the baby's incessant crying, Patricia could feel her head begin to clear. Walking without purpose she found her way to the creek out back where a meadowlark trilled its bright, clear song. She rested there for a while skipping stones along the surface of the rippling water. They skittered away like so many petty concerns.

Feeling better, she meandered back up toward the corrals. Hoping to be fed, the emus flocked to where she stopped at the fence. She reached out to scratch one on the top of its head. "Hello, my fine feathered friend," she said in a voice surprisingly not only sane but also congenial.

A calico kitten that the kids had named Tiger rubbed

up against her leg mewling for attention. Patricia stooped to pick it up. She rubbed her face in the softness of its long fur and was rewarded with a low purr of delight. Kicking a pebble under her toe, she headed back to the house. Cameron had been right. All she needed was a little space to herself to rediscover that when all was said and done, life wasn't so bad after all.

Stepping into the house, Patricia felt the seed of suspicion sprout in her heart. It was altogether too quiet. From experience she knew that particular sound held more potential for danger than the noisy reverberations of sibling squabbles and roughhousing. The messy kitchen floor would have to wait. Patricia was determined to find out just what was going on.

After discerning that Amy was not in her crib or her room, Patricia was drawn to the bathroom by the soft sound of running water. The door was slightly ajar. She pushed it open and peered in.

There she discovered her foreman squatting next to the tub, up to his elbows in bubble bath. Looking as content as an aristocrat who had finally found competent help, her daughter was giggling and splashing water all down the front of his flannel shirt. There appeared to be more water on the floor than in the tub.

How the man managed to look sexy in such a setting was beyond her, but with his shirt open and the muscles of his legs straining against the tight denim of his jeans, it was the first word to come to her mind. A wet lock of his blond hair sagged over his forehead. She'd seen puppy dogs left out in the rain all night that looked drier than Cameron did at the moment.

"Here, let me help you," she said, stepping into the room with her old air of confidence.

Cameron thought her smile as welcome as the sun on an overcast day. Careful not to slip on the water, Patricia leaned over him and took a dry towel off the rack behind him. The action drew her shirt tight across her breasts, and he felt the stirring of his sexual response thrumming through his body.

Amy smacked the surface of the water with open hands.

"That's enough out of you, young lady," Patricia warned, but her tone of voice implied no real threat.

Cameron plucked the culprit from the water and handed her over to her mother. "Upsy-daisy," he intoned, disregarding the fact that she was dripping water all over him.

Patricia rubbed the girl gently with a fluffy towel, wrapped her in its soft folds and set her down. She hit the floor running. Off flew the towel as she shrieked with delight at the cool feel of air upon bare skin. The tepid bath had helped drop her temperature, and she was obviously feeling better. The pitter-patter of her feet as she raced down the hall and into her room was indeed a joyful noise.

As Patricia bent to mop up the excess water on the floor with the discarded towel, Cameron studied her luscious curves. When she straightened, they almost collided in the cramped space.

"I'm sorry," she apologized.

"I'm not."

Her heart skipped several beats. Pretending to ignore the comment, she reached for another towel and attempted to treat him like one of her boys. Maternally.

"Here, let me help you out of that wet shirt."

Cameron didn't put up a struggle. He shrugged the shirt off, allowing himself the luxury of being pampered by a beautiful woman. The feel of her rubbing that soft towel against his skin was sheer heaven. He closed his eyes and indulged all of his senses. She smelled like strawberries, and he had the strongest urge to see if she tasted of them, too. Fingertips traced with infinite care the scars mapping his chest.

"It's nothing," he assured her through lazy lashes.

Glittering, Patricia's eyes bespoke her concern. The towel fell between them in a puddle of pink terry cloth. Her hands splayed across his chest in a soft, tender motion more seductive than anything he'd ever been subjected to in his whole life. It was as if she were touching the very surface of his heart, bringing it back to life with the magic of her healing touch.

"I certainly wouldn't call that nothing. What in the world happened to you?"

"You wouldn't believe me."

It was a statement of fact rather than conjecture on his part. He had tried telling her of his past, but she had refused to believe him. That fact alone should have been enough to break off the dangerous look of longing that passed between them. It was as electrically charged as the day she had fallen into his arms and both had been so shocked by the intensity of their reaction to each other. A couple of weeks of close contact had done nothing to lessen the sparks arcing between them like a direct short circuit. If anything, that stored energy had built up to atomic-bomb proportions.

But Cameron wasn't thinking of the fallout that was destined to follow when he stifled her gasp with a kiss. To his delight she did indeed taste of fresh berries and the essence of all good things in life—sunshine and promises and fulfillment. He told himself it was not a roaring in his ears he heard but simply the gurgle of water draining from the tub. His heart was hammering so loudly against his chest that it was hard to differentiate.

He deepened the kiss. Patricia responded fully to his demands, coiling her arms around his neck and melting against him. They fit together perfectly, as if God had knowingly made them for each other. Her hands riffled through his hair as she had been longing to do for so very long. This moment had been destined from the first minute their eyes had locked. Both had resisted to no avail. There was a savage sweetness in the mutual capitulation to forces beyond their control. Desire too long suppressed could no longer be denied.

In the most unlikely place for romance, they discovered the depth of their passion. Surprise widened both pairs of eyes simultaneously. Lips parted with the greatest of reluctance, and they regarded each other suspiciously.

Patricia had been married before and was the mother of three children. It hadn't occurred to her that a simple kiss could have such an impact on her. True, her relationship with Hadley had been based more on friendship and a desire to get out from under her father's control than on passion, but she had never considered their love life lacking. It had been comfortable if not dynamic. Patricia had always thought if she were ever to marry again, it would be that same comfort she would seek.

In the space of a magical moment, all that changed forever. Cameron's kiss opened a window on a world hitherto unknown to her. A world of breathless anticipation and unquenchable desire. Weak in the knees, Patricia felt light-headed. Blood was pulsating through her body in frightening palpitations. And the crazy thing about it was that she longed for more.

"Wow!" she uttered without thinking.

"Wow is right."

Cameron was looking at Patricia like she was some kind of beautiful sorceress who had cast a spell upon him, relegating the memory of any number of satisfying sexual encounters to the realm of junior high crushes. The blood coursing through his veins was hot and volatile. It took every ounce of self-control that he had to rein in his urge to take this woman right on the linoleum floor. The look smoldering in those wide, brown eyes told him she would not resist. Cameron understood that what he was feeling was far more than simple lust. Although he was not ready to give that feeling a name just yet, he knew that it was complicated by unresolved deception on his part. He needed time to sort it all out before things got completely out of hand.

"I'd better get back to work," he said in a voice too deep and husky to conceal how moved he was by the encounter.

"Yes, I suppose you should."

Their words implied that nothing had changed between them. Patricia was happy to play along with Cameron's pretense that their old adversarial relationship between boss and hired hand remained intact. Both of them knew it was a lie but desperately needed to pretend otherwise. They stepped away from each other, feeling less awkward with each other than with their own respective feelings. Both toyed with the same burning question. If a simple kiss had this kind of effect upon them, what would happen if things were carried any further?

Chapter Eleven

Lately Cameron's mind kept wandering back to the old sinkhole where he had first learned to swim. He had been no older than Kirk when he had turned a blind eye to the danger signs posted about, plunged in headfirst, and struck out in a comical dog paddle. It reminded him of the precarious position in which he found himself now. Though Patricia had posted warnings all around her heart and her home, Cameron found himself wading a little deeper into treacherous, emotional waters with each passing day. All of a sudden it seemed he was in it up to his neck.

Being home only strengthened his resolve to restore the Triple R to the ranch his grandfather had envisioned. Spencer Wade had stained the surrounding rocks red with his blood, tying future generations to this land. The fact that Patricia seemed to understand the intrinsic value of connecting her own family to this special place made Cameron feel both close to her and sorry for her.

He knew how hard it would be for her to give up claim to this magical place.

It was not pity, however, that had brought their lips together in the most sensual kiss he had ever experienced. A kiss like that brought a whole new meaning to the concept of foreplay. It lingered in his mind, suggesting a passion in Patricia that he had hitherto only imagined. The memory alone clouded rational thinking and left him in a permanent state of arousal.

Cameron could no more pretend that kiss had never happened than he could pretend indifference for this woman and her family. How he had become so quickly enmeshed in the daily drama of their lives was beyond him, but just as Patricia had warned him, he had become more than just a hired hand to the children. He had become their hero and their friend.

A dicey combination in the best of circumstances.

A few days ago he had been kicking the dust, unequivocally stating that he was a real cowboy, and the next he'd found himself playing nursemaid to a sick baby. Nursemaid, chauffeur, chicken wrangler. Cameron doubted whether his grandfather would be pleased with the ignominious duties his descendant had carved out for himself.

Friday was a teacher workday, and the children were thrilled with the prospect of spending the whole day unfettered by academic demands upon their time. As they lounged about watching television, Patricia handed her foreman his paycheck over breakfast.

The coffee in Cameron's mouth turned suddenly bitter. He pushed it away.

"Take it," she said, jutting out her chin proudly. "It's honest money, and you earned it. Far more, if the truth were known."

Looking around himself, Cameron felt suddenly ashamed. The faded kitchen wallpaper was beginning to curl in the corners, the linoleum in front of the sliding-glass door in back was spotted by years of direct sunlight, the children's T-shirts were growing smaller and thinner with each washing, and he wondered when the last time was that the lady of the house had bought anything pretty for herself. He started to protest that he didn't want her money, but something glimmering in those beautiful eyes of hers stayed his hand.

There's a difference between pride and prideful, Son, his mother had once told him. But until he'd looked into the depths of Patricia's eyes, he never fully understood what she had meant.

"Thanks," he said, folding the check in two and stuffing it into his shirt pocket.

Its weight felt leaden next to his heart.

"Hey, Mom, don't forget that I need a new pair of jeans," Johnny interjected over the mouthful of sugarcoated cereal he was eating like candy.

There was no denying it. His little ankles peeked out from the patched pair he was wearing. They were his play clothes, but the reality was that his school clothes were in little better shape.

Hearing her tired sigh, Johnny hastened to assure his mother, "It don't really matter."

"Doesn't," she automatically corrected.

As a child Patricia had taken for granted the things her own children lacked now. Things like fashionable clothes, expensive toys, vacations and spending money. The kind of things that other kids notice—and comment on. Things her parents would gladly provide them if only she would put aside her foolish pride, go home and submit herself to her father's tyrannical control for the rest of her life.

"And, yes, it does matter," she said. "A fine-looking boy like you needs to look nice for school. We'll just have to make a trip into town today. Amy's no longer contagious, and the drive'll do us all some good."

"You'll come too, won't you, Cameron?" asked Johnny. The excitement in his voice dented both his mother's and his idol's heart.

"You certainly deserve some time off," Patricia ventured with a hesitant smile. There was no denying that the thought of spending the day with a man whose lips had claimed a part of her that she thought had died long, long ago was tempting indeed. And with the children along to chaperone, there was little need to worry about another breach of propriety.

Darn it.

Cameron's experience with women had led him to believe that the wisest course was to simply confine his relationships to the mutual satisfaction of sexual urges and to part before any real emotional damage could be inflicted upon him again. A cramped trip to town with a passel of kids wasn't exactly his idea of a good time. He was just about to say no, thank you, when his gaze locked with Patricia's. Unspoken was the remembrance of a kiss that had forged a mystical bond of intimacy between them. It was scandalous that a mere glance could be so explosive.

"I'd like that very much."

Cameron's voice sounded the way smooth whisky tastes sliding down a parched throat. Though not much of a drinking man, he suddenly felt the need to steady his nerves.

"I'll make room for everybody in my truck," he offered, standing up to go.

Feeling a tremor run through her, Patricia resisted the urge to reach out and catch herself. She locked her knees, tossed him an encouraging smile and took a deep breath as he left the room. If she wasn't mistaken, the scent of masculine pursuit lingered in the air like faint perfume. Heady, dangerous, intoxicating...

Cameron hadn't been thinking of family comfort when he'd bought his extended-cab pickup. He liked it because it gave him extra room to carry and protect his expensive equipment. That he spent so much of his time living in his vehicle hadn't made him opposed to paying for the added comfort, either. He'd heard it said that a man's vehicle was merely an extension of his ego, and it hadn't bothered him a whit to lay down hard cash to buy the most expensive, powerful pickup on the lot. When a man paid his due with blood and broken bones, Cameron figured he deserved to have something to show for it. And he was determined to have more than just a fancy vehicle by the time he was done dealing. The Triple R still remained the ultimate prize.

While Patricia got herself and everyone else ready, he cleared out the space behind the seat. By the time they strapped in the baby seat and buckled everyone in, Cameron was surprised how happy he was feeling. He remembered how as a child he had loved those infrequent trips to town and how much penny candy could be bought with a handful of spare change.

The line of telephone poles alongside the dirt road that they were traveling stretched into an eternity of blue sky and looked like so many crucifixes connected. The boys chattered about things as inconsequential as

who would win in a fight between Superman and Spi-
derman, Amy cooed in delight as they crested each
swell in the road, Patricia basked in the warmth of the
sunshine through the windows, and Cameron enjoyed
feeling part of something very special—a family.

He was glad that Patricia didn't feel the need to en-
gage in small talk. Spectacular vistas and the feeling of
belonging made the miles speed by. Before Cameron
knew it, he was pulling into the outskirts of town.

Nestled idyllically in the Wind River Mountains, the
tight-knit community of Lander had changed little as
far as he could tell, since the day he'd left to make his
mark upon the world. He hung a proverbial Main, passing by Cindy's Diner where gossip had always traveled
faster than the speed of e-mail, past the high school that
to him had always looked more like a prison than an
institution of higher learning, and by the bank where
the only glimmer of compassion his father had ever
been able to discern was in the loan officer's one glass
eye.

Stopping in front of the local grocery store, he suggested, "Why don't you let me take the boys clothes
shopping while you and Amy go and pick up some
groceries?"

"You don't have to do that," Patricia protested.
"Isn't there something you'd like to do for yourself
while we're in town?"

"Only a phone call or two to make," he replied,
thinking of his agent and wondering if he was any
closer to signing a contract than when he had been laid
up in the hospital.

He knew his doctor would be amazed at his recuper-
ative powers. Fresh air, blue skies, physical labor and
some honest-to-goodness home cooking had done more

for him than any prescribed therapy. Of course, staying off bulls didn't hurt any, either. Cameron was surprised how little he missed the arena. The glamour, the glory, the adrenaline-packed thrills seemed tawdry somehow when held beside the picture that presented itself in front of the local grocery store. That of a contented man helping a woman and children out of a pickup.

When his hand touched hers and Patricia smiled into his eyes, Cameron felt the desire to kiss her again. And again. And again.

"We'll meet you back at the truck in about forty-five minutes," he told her.

She pressed a worn fifty-dollar bill into the palm of his hand. "Here," she said firmly. "You should be able to get a couple pairs of cheap jeans for both boys with this. And if it isn't enough, I'll make up the difference later."

Cameron slipped the money into his pocket. "I'm sure it'll be enough."

Watching her boys race across the street in their new clothes, Patricia knew she should have been mad. But the look of pure excitement blazing on their faces made it impossible to feel anything but gratitude for the man who had obviously overspent her self-imposed limit. Johnny and Kirk were sporting new boots, fashionable jeans and shirts, and expensive cowboy hats. Not the straw variety that harried mothers were badgered into buying at the local carnival, the kind that wore out in a couple of day's play, but the genuine article. She couldn't remember the boys looking happier.

"I hope you don't mind my picking up a few extra little things," Cameron said. "But we ran into a heck of a sale. They were practically giving stuff away, Patricia.''

Having grown to love the way her name rolled off his tongue like poetry, she bit the inside of her cheek to refrain from saying anything to damper the boys' enthusiasm. And to keep from spilling tears of appreciation. "I can see that."

Puzzled by unshed tears glistening in those beautiful eyes of hers, Cameron added feebly, "There's just enough left over for a couple of ice cream cones."

Squirming beneath the warmth of the look Patricia gave him, he felt relief flood his senses. For a minute there he thought she was going to demand he return the goods. And that would have hurt him worse than she could have imagined. The looks of pure joy on those boys' faces when he had loaded up the counter had given a new meaning to the old adage about it being better to give than to receive. Certainly what he'd received from them was without price.

"And this is from me out of my paycheck," he said, handing her a small sack. "Hope it fits all right."

Inside was the frilliest little girl dress Patricia had ever seen. Red-and-white-dotted Swiss adorned with enough ribbons to make Minnie Pearl blush, it was the type of dress a doting father would bestow upon the apple of his eye. The kind of thing that Patricia wished Hadley had bought his daughter. Unfortunately, the thought would never have crossed his preoccupied mind. She pulled the tiny garment from the sack and held it up to her own heart.

"Amy will love it," she assured him. *Almost as much as I do.*

"How do I look, Mom?" Kirk asked, throwing out his thin chest in an attempt to burst his buttons.

"You both look very handsome."

"As handsome as Cameron?" Johnny inquired with a hopeful grin.

"Almost," Patricia said, taking a moment to lose herself in his fathomless blue eyes. The intimacy of his returning gaze made her feel breathless and expectant. He was close enough that his heady masculine scent was able to work its spell on her, and for a brief, magical minute Patricia could actually envision him as a permanent part of her life.

"Almost," she repeated, breaking the enchantment of the moment with a generous smile. "Give yourself a few years, boys, and you'll be just as heartbreakingly good-looking as him."

Lately the boys had both taken to imitating Cameron's mannerisms, and the truth was they looked so alike standing there with their respective thumbs hitched in their front pockets that it was uncanny. Anyone passing them on the street would have assumed they were bonded by blood.

Cameron swelled up in his own shirt much like Kirk had. He found Patricia's kind words an uncomfortable fit. "Let's go get that ice cream," he suggested, shrugging off any awkwardness he was feeling.

The offer met with everyone's hearty approval.

In addition to serving the best malts in town, the Dairy Barn boasted "fifties charm." As long as autumn held to snowless skies, high school part-timers bustled out to waiting customers' cars on roller skates. The children loved the click of metal upon cement and the anticipation of calamitous falls.

As Cameron ordered hamburgers, fries and chocolate malts all around, Patricia enjoyed the questionable ambiance of the place. Considering that they were the only

vehicle in the lot, she thought it odd that the next cus-
tomer pulled in beside them just as close as possible.

An old lady with a tight perm and blue hair peered
at the raucous bunch in the pickup beside her. Patricia
recognized her as Mildrid Coleman, Elliott's mother.
Terrified that she might lose her middle-aged son to the
young Widow Erhart, Mildrid clucked her disapproval
whenever Elliott stopped to talk to her on the street.

Patricia groaned to see the dowager of Lander, Wyoming, rolling down her window to take a long gander
at the competition. Once she had made certain of Patricia's identity, Mildrid fixed a sanctimonious expression upon her face and received the younger woman's
friendly wave with stony antipathy.

"Looks like a poodle sniffing a turd," was Cameron's candid observation.

Sorry that Mildred had overheard the comment, Patricia did her best to keep from laughing. Not wanting
to set a bad example for her boys, she bit the inside of
her cheek as the older lady wrestled with the manual-
style window handles of her vintage-model car. Indignation puffing from her exhaust pipe, she spun out of
the lot before the waitress could so much as take her
order.

"I feel like I've just been caught skipping class back
in high school," Patricia said with a careless little
shrug.

"Wouldn't doubt that old biddy's probably off to tell
the principal." Cameron bit his nails in mock horror.
"Hope she says hi to Joe for me."

The hands on the clock of life stopped for a moment
and miraculously turned backward. Encounters with
school administration had been so familiar to him that
he eventually had come to refer to the principal by his
first name. Rumor had it that the teachers were so weary

of Cameron's attitude they had gotten together and decided to pass him just so they wouldn't have to deal with him for another year.

The pretty teenager who brought their orders scanned the occupants in the vehicle. Patricia noticed how her gaze lingered on Cameron and heard her infatuated sigh as she took her leave. Obviously it wasn't every day such a fine-looking male specimen graced this establishment, and Patricia was pretty sure that she had been sent with specific instructions from the other girls inside to take careful inventory before reporting back.

As the children wolfed down their hamburgers, the adults in the front seat shared a smile and a packet of ketchup. Patricia swished a fry in the sauce and fed it to Amy. She couldn't remember the last time she'd eaten out, and said so.

Looking around at the gritty parking lot, Cameron wondered when Patricia had last eaten a meal in a nice restaurant—without the kids.

"If I asked you out to dinner, could you arrange for a baby-sitter?" he asked with feigned nonchalance.

The question caught Patricia off guard. Cameron seemed to have a lot of disposable income for a man working for slave wages. The groceries he had bought, the excessive spending on the children's clothes, the fancy pickup, and now the offer to take her out to dinner. It just didn't add up. He may have admitted to being on a nostalgia trip, but he'd said nothing about being independently wealthy.

"If you don't watch out, this little sentimental journey into your past is going to end up costing you instead of making you money."

Cameron's laughter broke down all her reservations with a rumbling heartiness. "You're the first woman

I've ever met who worried I'd spend too much on her. Trust me," he cajoled seductively, "dinner won't break me."

Patricia experienced a rush of excitement at the thought of spending an evening alone with this man. With no car seat to separate them, she might just be tempted to snuggle up beside him like a schoolgirl in the throes of a crush.

"Are you talking about a real date?" she asked.

Good Lord, the question sounded so silly and juvenile to her own ears that she again felt transported back in time to her awkward high school days.

"Yeah, like a real date," Cameron responded with a boyish smile that erased years off his heart.

"I'd say yes."

Challenge flashed in her dark eyes, and Cameron wished that he'd acted upon the whim he'd had back in the clothing shop where he had paid outrageous prices to outfit the boys. An expensive dress in the window had caught his eye, and he had thought how lovely Patricia would look in the soft satin folds of its classic design. But a gift of clothing to a woman felt too personal. It hinted at the promise of an intimate, lasting relationship, and as much as he was presently enjoying himself, Cameron wasn't ready to commit to anything just yet other than regaining control of the Triple R.

"Tomorrow night then," he said.

Patricia polished off the last of her fries and checked her watch. "I'm afraid it's time to go home and feed the birds."

"Sonuva—" Kirk piped up in the back seat.

Patricia gasped. "What did you say?"

To his mother's horror Kirk repeated himself louder and more clearly.

"Where did you hear such language?" she demanded.

"Cameron calls the birds that all the time," he explained, and looked to his brother for support.

"He's got special names for all of them that I'd never even heard of before. Wanna hear 'em?" Johnny offered helpfully.

Cameron hadn't blushed in years, but his face turned as red as the ketchup on Amy's collar as he hurried to do damage control. "I didn't realize they paid any attention to what I mumble under my breath."

Patricia didn't have to say a word to make her displeasure felt. She had expressed her concerns about his suitability as a role model right up front, and though he had resented the assertion at the time, it seemed she had a point. The look she leveled at him would have crushed the most hardened criminal.

"Well, boys, I guess I owe you and your mom an apology. It's been so long since I've been around young, innocent ears that I forgot myself. Tell you what," he said, pausing to stroke his mustache, "how about if we come up with some different names on the way home. Names your mother'd approve of. I bet good old Dr. Seuss could help us out. I seem to remember a lazy bird by the name of Mayzie who left all her nesting responsibilities to Horton who eventually hatched a Who."

There was a decided undercurrent to the allusion. Having watched how the female emus dominated the males, Cameron found the parallel disturbing. If for some reason the lady birds took a dislike to a fellow, they picked on him unmercifully, running him ragged. And if they were able to corner him, they would gang up and peck at him until he was covered with bald spots. The spectacle gave new meaning to the term hen-pecked. The poor guy was then left to incubate the egg and raise the offspring while the female was off looking for another mate.

"And," he continued, trying to dismiss the image from his mind, "I believe there was a plain girlie bird named Gertrude McFuzz who was a little bit jealous of the fancy feathers of a pretty little gal by the name of Lolla-Lee-Loo."

"And don't forget the grinch who stole Christmas," Patricia supplied.

Cameron didn't much care for that particular reference. He knew that when Patricia finally came to understand that he had his sights set on buying back the ranch, that irascible, old grinch would look like Santa Claus next to him. *Grinch* was certain to be the nicest word she might use to describe him. Hoping to break the news to her over dinner, he wondered whether the lady's choice of vernacular might not make his own breach of discretion seem rather tame.

Chapter Twelve

Pirouetting in front of the full-length mirror in her bedroom, Patricia gave herself a mixed review. Though her hair was in need of a ruthless trim by a good stylist, it was nonetheless glossy and full. Her dress might have been a little faded, but it showed off her figure well and made her feel younger and prettier than she had in years. The last time she had been on a real date was when she was still in her teens, and she felt every bit as excited as when she had gone to the prom.

She looked at her hands and wished there were some way to make them look presentable. As a girl, her father had inspected her nails once a week. Patricia was certain that Roland D'Winter would be aghast that her once lovely hands now looked like those of his gardener. The best she could do with them was to trim the nails evenly and push back the cuticles. Be that as it may, she felt certain by now that Cameron Wade wasn't the kind of man who put much stock in the things that her father had.

It was a startling revelation. Standing there in her bedroom, she suddenly realized that a good deal of what was stopping her from pursuing a relationship with her foreman was the fear that he was like her father. On the surface, there were certain overt similarities. Both were strong, uncompromising men, but Cameron lacked the domineering side that had ruined her relationship with her father and encouraged her to seek out someone less demanding and more malleable as a mate. In his inter-actions with both her and the children, Cameron seemed willing to allow them their own individuality and en-couraged a sense of self-reliance that Roland D'Winter would have found threatening. Nor did Cameron feel the need to belittle those around him like her father did to make himself look important and all knowing. The boys seemed to grow inches with just one of Cameron's well-timed compliments. And unlike her stern father, Cameron liked to laugh. So warm and contagious, the sound of his frequent laughter resonated in Patricia's heart.

At the sound of the pickup rolling into the driveway, Patricia took a final twirl in front of the mirror and bid her worries farewell for the evening. That would be Cameron returning with their baby-sitter. A high school girl with her sights on being valedictorian, Jewel Har-grove was well named and always in demand as a baby-sitter. She had several younger siblings and a knack for entertaining Kirk and Johnny without insulting their budding sense of independence. Patricia felt lucky to have booked her on such short notice.

"You sure look pretty, Mom," Johnny commented as his mother came down the stairs.

"Yes, you do," Cameron echoed.

His eyes flashed with desire and something else that

Patricia couldn't quite put her finger on. Could that possibly be possessiveness glimmering in the depths of those sky-blues?

Kirk broke the mood by hitting his brother over the head with a throw pillow on the couch. Patricia took it away and handed it to Cameron.

"You boys be good now, you understand? I don't want to come home to a disaster area," she chided gently.

They nodded together, and she went on to give Jewel specific instructions about their bedtime, their eating habits and their television privileges. Cameron paid no attention. His concentration was fixed upon the needlework pillow in his hands and the words that had been so patiently stitched there.

"A house is made of walls and beams; a home is made of love and dreams."

Those simple words pulled at his heart. For the first time since he'd set the course for recovering the Triple R, Cameron was besieged by self-doubt. What if a silly pillow held the answer to what he'd spent a lifetime searching for? Was it possible that what he was trying to buy back was neither in the lumber nor the land? Having always connected the warmth this family shared with the loving glow of his own memories of growing up here, the possibility that what he was trying to recapture could not be purchased with any amount of money was more than just a little disquieting. It was earth-shattering.

Maintaining that she didn't care whether it embarrassed them or not, Patricia insisted on a parting kiss from each of her children. "Have fun," they called out as Cameron helped Patricia into her coat. The simple courtesy made her feel so cherished that it was difficult for her to resist kissing him right there in front of everyone.

Amy had no such qualms. She held her arms up to Cameron and demanded a goodbye kiss. No man could have resisted that charming pout framed with the stain of fruit juice. Eyes the color of aspen leaves in spring were shaded by a set of eyelashes that grown women would kill for. Taking Amy into his arms, Cameron reveled in the warmth of the kiss she placed upon his cheek.

"Don't you let those big brothers of yours boss you around any," he told her.

The obvious affection in his voice made Patricia wish she could hold the moment forever in time. Such were the simple things that make life a joyous daily adventure.

A moment later they were on their way, and finding themselves suddenly alone, they became tongue-tied in each other's company. Cameron was grateful that unlike so many women he knew, Patricia didn't feel the need to fill the silence with idle chatter. When he pulled over to point out a herd of elk on the horizon, she slid naturally over to his side to peer out his window.

He tore his gaze from the wildlife outside to linger on the beauty beside him. A simple turn of his head brought their lips close. The last time he had kissed her, Amy had been a sudsy bystander. They had both been so shocked by the intensity of that kiss that they had remained dazed in its aftermath. This time as he lowered his mouth to hers, Cameron was determined to make a slow, thorough exploration of the feelings that were threatening to raze good sense and everything he'd ever worked for.

Heat burgeoned through Patricia like a fireball exploding her universe apart. She had tried telling herself that she had only imagined the impact of the previous kiss. She had lain awake at night rationalizing her feelings away, telling herself that she had been so deeply affected only because it had been so very long since she had been with a man. But such feeble logic was useless before the conflagration that burned away any semblance of resistance to the demands of Cameron's mouth. Caught in a maelstrom of emotions threatening to sweep her away, she clung to the strong column of his neck as if it were a life preserver. Her fingertips riffled through his blond hair, so fine it felt like satin to the touch. It was just long enough to grab by twin handfuls and draw him closer yet. After an eternity, when the kiss ended, they were both breathing so hard that the windows had begun to fog over.

There was no denying the chemistry between them. Together they were as flammable as kerosene and matches. Their eyes met and held for one amazing instant, mirroring the mutual longing to consummate their love in broad daylight right there on the side of the road. But when a semi whooshed past them, spitting gravel in its wake, Patricia took one of Cameron's hands into hers and squeezed it hard. "We'd better get going," she murmured.

"In a minute," he replied, dipping his head to deposit another kiss upon the hollow of her throat.

"Mmm…"

Throwing her head back, Patricia felt the last of her resistance evaporate like a raindrop hitting a hot window. Neither a child nor an innocent virgin, she knew exactly what it was she wanted. And she wanted this man. For the moment. Forever.

That Cameron wanted her, too, was not the question.
But if he sullied her reputation, could Patricia and her
family survive the scorn of the good people who inhab-
ited this conservative rural community?

"You're right. It's time to get going," he agreed so
suddenly that it was jarring. Obvious frustration written
on his features contradicted his words.

Patricia felt confused, but she acquiesced to logic
without argument. She smoothed out her skirt and ran
a shaky hand through her disheveled riot of hair in a
vain attempt to gather her wits about her.

Cameron rolled down his window and allowed fresh
air to fill his lungs. Keeping one arm firmly around
Patricia's shoulders, he refused her access to the other
side of the truck. She did not fight him, but instead
rested her head against his chest and took comfort in
the sound of his heart beating so steady and strong next
to her ear. They sat there for a while longer thus en-
twined, entranced by the magic surrounding them. As
the golden sun kissed the earth adieu, the red clay
blushed a shade deeper. It seemed perfectly logical that
this was the very spot where Adam had been formed
from a mixture of dry dust and God's spittle.

Patricia ran her hands along Cameron's ribs. Though
the story of Eve being brought into being from Adam's
side had always seemed rather sexist to her, suddenly
the thought of God providing soul mates for his lonely
creatures gave her a sense of deep comfort and serenity.

A haunting love song played on the radio as they
drove the remainder of the way into town. There was
only one fancy restaurant in town, and it wasn't all that
nice. Still it boasted a modest dance floor, and to a
woman who hadn't been on a date for over a decade, it
seemed like a little piece of heaven. Not having to fix

dinner, period, was a treat in itself. Patricia mentioned how simply being waited on seemed strange.

"I'm warning you," Cameron chided with a devilish wink. "If you reach over and cut up my steak for me, I'm going to slap your hand."

Patricia giggled at the image. How wonderful it was to put aside her mommy persona for an evening and be in the company of a man handsome enough for a Hollywood set. She felt truly lighthearted for the first time in ages. Bills and housework and homework and sibling squabbles awaited her when she returned like Cinderella from her night out, but until the clock struck the fateful hour, Patricia was determined to enjoy herself. She refused to think a single depressing thought.

Like how soon Cameron would be moving on and leaving a hole in her heart twice the size of Wyoming.

He poured her a glass of wine and watched the tension drain from her features. She was a very pretty woman. Cameron couldn't help thinking what a complete knockout she would be with a new dress and a fresh haircut. Gazing into Patricia's refreshingly open face, he had second thoughts. A beautician could do little to improve upon her simple perfection.

"You're beautiful." The look in his eyes echoed the compliment.

Patricia smiled hesitantly, wondering whether to believe him. Hadley had never been much for sweet talk. Her father had said flattery was the devil's work and allowed none in his home. She had to consciously refrain from discounting Cameron's praise.

"Thank you," she said simply. To her surprise, the simple acknowledgment made her feel sexy and desirable.

Seeing how uncomfortable Patricia was at receiving

his compliments, Cameron again found himself wondering what kind of man her husband had been. He couldn't have been blind to her beauty. Perhaps he was the insecure type who feared such praise would give her the confidence to leave him.

Cameron was taken with this woman. No doubt about it. His past brimmed with failed relationships with women wanting no more from him than what his notoriety and pocketbook could provide them, but Patricia had no such motivation for bestowing the warmth of her smile upon him. Unwilling to accept his claim to fame, her attempt to melt the ice pack that had held his heart captive for so long could not be motivated by greed or self-promotion. That such a woman could like him just for himself was a wondrous thing.

Filled like a vessel to overflowing, with a rare sense of happiness, Cameron longed for the sound of her laughter. Toward that end, he cracked a silly joke about the birds that blighted his life with their noise and stench.

"Ah, but they love you," she insisted. "The way the mammas have taken to you, I'd lay odds that at least one chick will imprint with you at hatching time. That is, if you'd care to stick around till the first of the year."

Patricia tossed the comment out as nonchalantly as one would mention the weather or some other such mundane subject. But her hands gave away her real feelings. They were shaking ever so slightly as she lifted the wineglass to her lips.

Cameron felt his heart leap to his throat at the offer. She wanted him to stay. Needed him. For more than just maintenance work he suspected. But rather than show the depth of his feelings, he focused instead upon her remark about imprinting.

"I draw the line at playing mamma hen to lost chicks," he said.

Patricia worried her lower lip between her teeth. There was more than one way to take that assertion. She related to the image of a poor little hatchling following Cameron around. For some reason he was just the kind of man who naturally made one feel safe, protected—and cherished.

"Why, Cameron Wade, you old—!"

The oath trailed off and was swallowed up by the hubbub of other conversations wafting through the room amid the aroma of delicious food. Patricia looked alarmed. Was someone going to make trouble for them on such a pleasant evening?

A big fellow with a ruddy complexion pushed his way through the maze of tables and chairs. He stood before Cameron and took a long moment to size him up. Then he grasped his hand and began pumping it up and down like a piston.

"How've ya been?" he demanded in a booming voice. "Glad to see you're back home at last. We're all awful proud of ya, boy. Awful proud."

Meeting the man's gaze head-on, Cameron seemed surprised at the sincerity he found there.

As a buzz passed from table to table like a bee passing from one blossom to another, people started staring. And pointing.

"That's Cameron Wade," whispered one.

"The bull rider?"

Another cowboy, a younger version of the first, stepped up to the table and shook Cameron's hand as well. "Surprised you ain't wearing that championship buckle. I sure would if it was me."

Patricia's mouth fell open. A drop of wine fell upon

the white tablecloth, staining it red with shame. The blush on her cheeks was a perfect match.

"You ever get a hankering to move back here," offered a gentleman at the table next to them, "I've got a nice piece of property along the river that's prime ranch land. I'm getting too old to run the place myself."

Cameron looked as startled as Patricia. After spending years imagining he had something to prove to the people living here, it came as quite a shock to discover that they seemed genuinely happy for his success. When he finished accepting praise from all around, he turned to her and softly said, "I tried telling you, but you wouldn't listen."

Words failed her. Never before had Patricia felt such a complete and utter fool. He hadn't lied to her after all. She had spent so much time worrying that she might fall for another man made out of the same flimsy cloth from which Hadley had been cut that it hadn't occurred to her to believe Cameron's claim.

Her own words came back to haunt her.

If it's any consolation, I had a heck of a time myself selecting you from among all those other rodeo stars who applied for the job—and the movie stars, too. How embarrassing for a man of your stature to be working here of all places. How humbling!

How humbling indeed.

"Why?" she uttered through a haze of confusion. Why would a rodeo superstar hire himself out as a lowly ranch hand? What was his ulterior motive?

"I'll answer all your questions in a moment," Cameron assured her. "But right now I'd very much like the pleasure of a dance with the prettiest woman in the place."

He took her by the hand and led her to the dance

floor. Patricia was too stunned to do anything but follow. Feeling lightheaded, she leaned against him. His arms went around her, and she mumbled apologetically. "I'm afraid I'm not much of a dancer."

"Hush," he whispered back, and she felt the warmth of his breath raise goose bumps against the nape of her neck.

She did as she was told, swaying mindlessly to the beat of a slow, hurting song that wrung her heart out like an old dishcloth. The end was coming, but Patricia was willing to forestall it for the length of a song.

Cameron felt her shudder in his arms. A single tear fell upon his shoulder, and he felt its weight upon his soul.

"Ah, honey," he implored, standing quite still. The other dancers moved around them, covertly eavesdropping on the drama unfolding in their very midst. "Don't cry. I'm not worth it."

She stroked his face as if it were the most precious gift on earth. "I am so sorry I doubted you. So terribly sorry."

Cameron had relished the thought of the day he was going to make this woman eat crow. Now that it had arrived, he took no satisfaction from it. His heart felt like someone was squeezing it. Hard.

"It's all right," he crooned softly, hoping she would be half as generous when she heard the rest of the story. Right there in the middle of the dance floor, he kissed her so tenderly, so thoroughly that a little boy sitting at a table with his parents was moved to exclaim with the loud enthusiasm of an innocent voyeur, "Wow!"

Everyone within earshot laughed. Everyone except a certain man who had obviously had too much to drink.

He forced his way to the dance floor and tapped Cameron on the shoulder.

"I heard rumors it was you who was working for the bird lady, but I couldn't bring myself to believe that any self-respecting cowboy worth his salt would sink so low as to hand in his prize belt buckle for a Colonel Sanders hat and apron."

The music had stopped, and the dancers hurried to make their way back to the safety of their chairs. Cameron smelled the whisky on the man's breath and tried turning him away with equal measures of forcefulness and civility.

"You're drunk, mister," he stated, taking Patricia by the elbow and steering her off the dance floor. "And since I don't particularly want any trouble tonight, I'd suggest you go and sober up and count yourself a lucky man in the morning."

Patricia flinched as the lout stepped between them and bodily blocked her path. He may have been drunk, but he was also very big and clearly intent on making himself look big by challenging the town's local hero. On more occasions than she cared to remember Hadley had sloshed the bottle dry, but he had never been a mean drunk. The hatred written on this man's hardened features made Patricia feel very sorry for any woman unfortunate enough to be in this fellow's life.

"Come off it, Dick," called a voice from the crowd. "The last thing you need right now is another strike against you before you go to court."

Ignoring his friend's admonition, Dick taunted Cameron with the same term the rodeo announcer used with admiration on the circuit. "Come on, Big Man. I dare you to take a swing at me," he poked his intended victim in the chest with his forefinger for added emphasis, "Chicken Man."

Cameron's voice was soft yet commanding as he told Patricia to "go sit down." She stepped aside and heard him offer the man a final warning. "Buddy, this is your last chance to walk away from here with all your teeth."

"Well, I guess it's true that big old dumb birds of a feather do stick together, Chicken Man!"

Rough and masculine, the sound of his laughter filled Patricia with primitive fear. "Let's go," she urged Cameron. "You don't have to respond to this big ape for me."

Dick smelled her fear and was spurred on by it. He continued making a spectacle of himself by tucking his hands beneath his armpits and flapping his arms up and down. "Cluck, cluck, cluck, cluck..."

A muscle in Cameron's jaw jumped. His blue eyes turned the color of ice. "Let's go outside," he suggested with deadly calm. If it could be avoided, he'd just as soon not subject Patricia to any display of violence.

"But now I see the two of you together with my own eyes, I can understand your thinking better. It's a different kind of hen you're after, heh? Maybe there's far less bird bid'ness going on at the widow Erhart's place than monkey bid'n—"

Cameron didn't let him finish. It seemed the only way of ensuring the man shut his ugly mouth was by ramming his fist into it. Blood spewed in all directions. The unfortunate meddler staggered to his knees, holding his mouth. He spit a tooth into his open palms.

"Sum uf a—" he muttered. Only temporarily stunned, he flung himself at Cameron's ankles and knocked him to the ground.

A chair splintered beneath Cameron's weight as he fell upon it. The man was on top of him in an instant flailing his fists as if into a feather pillow. Cameron shifted beneath him, and the sound of Dick's fist connecting with the hardwood floor splintered in Patricia's ears. Though his agonizing groans left little doubt that he wanted no more to do with the famous bull rider, Cameron drove his point home with a solid upper cut.

The giant of a man lay sprawled on the floor like so much dirty water waiting to be mopped up. Parting to let Cameron pass, the crowd cheered.

He shrugged it off with the practiced nonchalance of a celebrity.

It was tempting to remain here and bask in the glow of mass admiration. Cameron had a sick feeling in his gut that the brawl he left behind was going to be nothing compared to the one awaiting him. The stiff set of Patricia's backbone as she preceded him outside told him he was in for the fight of his life.

Chapter Thirteen

Patricia applied an ice pack to Cameron's eye with clinical aloofness. She had remained pointedly quiet on the way home, not even putting up a token argument when he insisted on driving himself. Offering neither reprimands nor praise for his part in the altercation that had not only ruined a perfect evening but also left his right eye swelling and purple, she remained rooted to her side of the pickup.

As Cameron took the baby-sitter home, she checked on the children. They were fast asleep in their respective beds. Kirk's front tooth, which had been hanging on by a mere thread, was enshrined atop the kitchen table in the official family tooth-fairy jar, awaiting the traditional monetary exchange. Only after swapping a fifty-cent piece for the baby tooth did Patricia turn her attention to the man walking through the front door.

"Sit down," she commanded, grabbing an ice pack out of the freezer, "and let me have a look at that eye."

Though her ministrations were some consolation,

Cameron had hoped for something warmer than the professional-nursing routine to which Patricia subjected him. Having sacrificed his face in the defense of her honor, the least he expected was a kiss to make it feel better.

"Ouch!" he exclaimed, brushing her hand away. "Are you purposely trying to push that ice pack through the back of my head?"

"Sit still."

For all the sympathy he was getting, Patricia might as well have been removing the tiniest of slivers from a petulant child's finger. The full lips he had kissed just a short time ago had lost all their generosity. Pursing them as if holding back something distasteful, Patricia worked in silence, volunteering nothing of her thoughts.

"You can't possibly be mad to discover that I was telling you the truth all along," he scoffed.

The silence was deafening, as skeptical brown eyes burned a hole right through him. He knew better than to rush in where angels feared to tread, but even as a child Cameron could never leave well enough alone. He was the sort who took perverse pleasure in picking at a scab.

"If you'd care to remember back a week or so, you laughed in my face when I tried to tell you a little about myself."

Patricia rolled her son's baby tooth between her fingers and held it up to the light as if to examine it in detail. Squinting, she ventured her opinion.

"My boys may believe in the tooth fairy, but I don't. Things just don't stack up right. A big-name rodeo star signing on to work as a lowly hired hand out of the goodness of his heart? I'm not buying it, cowboy. Why, with all your winnings you could buy any ranch around here that you wanted.''

The light of sudden understanding dawned in Patricia's eyes. ''You want my ranch! That's your scam, isn't it?''

Cameron flinched from the word which evoked images of shysters, snake oil salesmen, bankers in pinstripes...and of all the fools taken in by them. First and foremost on the list was his own father, who had put his faith in the dubious good will of his long-time friend and personal banker. And then there was Patricia's dead husband who had apparently been taken in by every con artist within fifty miles of him.

Ignoring the tug at his conscience, he responded cryptically, ''I also told you about my ties to this place.''

Patricia eyed him with that same unblinking resolve that inevitably elicited the whole, unvarnished truth from her children.

''I care too much about the Triple R to see it falling down in disrepair,'' he felt compelled to add.

Patricia's hands went to her hips in indignation. Just because he had done more around this place in about a week than had been accomplished in the previous decade didn't give him the right to rub it in her face.

''In case you haven't noticed, this isn't the Triple R anymore. It's my home. Now, I'm only going to ask you one more time. What exactly are you after?''

Cameron's purpose was his own. He was here, of course, because this land, claimed by the sweat, blood and audacity of his grandfather, was his birthright. He was here because destiny demanded that he reclaim it and restore dignity to the Wade name. He was here because the realization of a twenty-year dream hinged on his presence.

Feeling as defensive as a choirboy caught drinking the communion wine, Cameron's first impulse was to come out swinging. But one glance into that gentle face and he suddenly lost his way around the fight. The hint of moisture glistening in eyes the color of fine scotch made him go as weak as Superman in the presence of kryptonite. The proud tilt of Patricia's jaw made her look as vulnerable as little Amy Leigh refusing to back down in the face of her big brothers' bullying. Cameron knew many women who could cry on cue if it got them what they wanted, but he searched his memory for a single one who could keep the tears from falling by sheer willpower alone.

Nope, this was a first.

Finding that he admired her a whole lot more than he did himself at the moment, Cameron realized he could no more stonewall this good woman than he could spit on his own mother's grave.

"Why exactly am I here?" he said dully, uncrossing his arms and taking a deep breath. "The truth is I came here to buy this ranch out from under you."

His words resonated in the room like the lingering sound of a death knell. Patricia's eyes widened in disbelief, and the hurt tangibly shimmering there sliced Cameron to the bone.

"I want to buy you out, Patricia," he said, meeting those wounded eyes directly. "I want to turn this place into the finest quarter-horse ranch in the whole state. I'm prepared to offer you a fair price. More than fair."

"And just when were you going to get around to telling me about all this?" Patricia asked through tight lips. "When you presented me with the receipt for the back taxes?"

Back taxes? So things were actually as bad as that.

Cameron knew that Patricia was struggling to make ends meet, but apparently her finances were even worse than he'd imagined. A month ago he would have taken advantage of this woman's dire straits without giving it a second thought. Now, however, he recoiled from the accusation as if from a rattlesnake.

"Of course not!" he protested, feeling like some mustache-twirling villain in an old-fashioned melodrama. "It's just that I've been waiting on a contract from my agent that may or may not materialize. The minute I was sure I had the money, I planned on making you a generous offer."

"'Fair, more than fair, generous'..." Patricia repeated his choice of adjectives with disdain. "I wonder if Judas used such discriminating words when he accepted his thirty pieces of silver."

Cameron threw up his hands at the comparison. "It's not like that," he protested.

"Yes, yes it is," she insisted, grabbing a stack of mail off the table and rifling through it with an intensity of purpose that was frightening to behold. "It's exactly like that, you manipulative son of a—wolf in sheep's clothing."

Finding what she was looking for, Patricia thrust a manila envelope beneath his nose. "Something came in the mail for you today. Probably that fat contract you've been waiting for. Take it and get out of here."

Cameron stared at the package she so ignominiously dropped in his lap. It was indeed from his agent, and from the size and weight of it, he guessed it to be good news.

"This could be a new start for us both," he suggested, his voice a harsh whisper in the stillness of the room.

He didn't want to leave. Not now. Not like this.

Until this very minute Cameron hadn't truly understood how much he had come to care for this woman
and her children. The thought of life devoid of their
presence stretched before him like a desolate road littered with empty beer bottles discarded by passersby
wasting their days on false, illusive dreams. It came as
quite a shock to him to discover that all he had been
seeking his whole life was right here in the same room
where his own parents had so openly displayed their
love. It had absolutely nothing to do with riding back
into town a big man, as he once had thought. It had
nothing to do with fame or money or all the glitz the
world had to offer. It had nothing to do with the land
that he held so precious.

It had everything to do with the woman standing before him.

All of his hopes and his dreams, desires and needs
were wrapped up in this precious woman who wanted
nothing more from him than a hasty farewell.

The realization that he loved her drilled him between
the eyes like a bullet. Grabbing her by the hand, he drew
her near. She pulled away as if fearing the contamina-
tion of his touch.

"Patricia," he implored, "I should have enough
money now to—"

"I don't want your money!" she yelled, certain that
her first impression had been right all along. He *was*
just like her father. Domineering, manipulative, shrewd.
Such men believed that everything in the world had a
price tag attached. Certain that money was more important than love, respect, trust or honesty, Roland
D'Winter thought his daughter and grandchildren could
be bought as easily as the blue-chip stocks he so dearly

prized. Cameron Wade was as dead wrong in assuming that money was the cure-all for everything as her father had been. Some things simply were not for sale—at any price.

I don't want your money!

Her words reverberated in Cameron's mind like a gunshot echoing off the canyon walls. Patricia was as different from the gold diggers of his past as heaven was from hell. He was a fool, so eager to hold on to his preconceived notions that he had risked losing the only chance of happiness life held out for him. With a woman such as this at his side, nothing could hold him back from becoming the man he was meant to be. Her children were already as dear to him as if they were his own, and the love he felt for Patricia was as undeniable as the wild beating of a heart straining against a chest too small to contain its savage song. With sudden clarity, Cameron knew he wanted nothing more than to be inexorably intertwined in their lives and to spend the rest of his days loving this amazing woman.

The intractable expression on Patricia's face, however, told him this was definitely not the best time to propose.

"We can make this work," he said with resolve that belied the quivering in his gut. Feeling like he was running uphill in dense sand, he implored, "It's not too late."

But there was no compromise in Patricia's eyes.

"Get out," she told him simply.

Patricia sat in the midst of a living room surrounded by a mountain of unmatched socks, the undisputed queen of mayhem. The days were growing shorter, and

the sun had set on more than one incomplete chore. It
was no use calling the boys back to make them finish
the job that they had so halfheartedly begun. Not when
she had only moments before played right into their
hands and banished them from the room. She jabbed a
needle angrily into the throw pillow whose reassuring
needlepoint message had sustained her through innu-
merable moves and the death of a husband. Half of its
stuffing lay in her lap, a casualty of the war her children
were waging upon the world ever since they had awakened to find Cameron Wade forever exiled from their
kingdom.

Their mother's responses to their relentless inquiries
as to why he had left without so much as a goodbye to
them were as enigmatic as they were curt. Not ones to
be put off lightly, they made their displeasure known in
a hundred less-than-subtle ways. Why, just this afternoon Patricia had been summoned to the principal's office to discuss the latest in a series of playground in-
fractions involving both her boys.

Lost in her thoughts, Patricia stabbed herself with the
needle she was using to mend the pillow her children
had used in their latest battle. She sucked the pearl of
blood from the tip of her index finger and found it as
bitter as the words of that sour-faced school psychiatrist
Mrs. Ebah. Far from the sympathetic, if not somewhat
resigned, attitude of the school principal, who was
within months of retiring, the woman whom the children secretly dubbed Mrs. Eyeballs was called upon to
state her textbook opinion. She began with a tight smile.

"Surely you're aware that boys their age desperately
need a strong male role model in their lives."

The woman's voice was as dry as rustling stalks of
withered corn.

"The fact that they are without a father, compounded by the um...er...serious challenges your family is facing, leads me to believe that Kirk and Johnny are engaging in what we in the field refer to as triangulation. That is, their acting out both in the classroom and on the playground is merely a ploy to gain your attention and draw the focus away from some very real issues."

Patricia had an overwhelming urge to demonstrate the difference between triangulation and strangulation to this dried-up old biddy who could no more read nonverbal signals than she could navigate her way through anything but a virtual relationship.

"The fact that they are victims of the cruel hand fate has dealt them does not necessarily mean that with regular counseling they cannot survive—"

Patricia could stand no more of the woman's idiotic psychobabble. "My children are not victims, Mrs. Ebah," she said coolly in a voice indicating that she personally thought psychologists and the devil went hand in hand. "And I have every intention that they will do far more than *survive* their days on this planet. They will *thrive* I assure you—without weekly trips to your office to discern any errors in the way I potty-trained them."

Standing up, Patricia ended the conference with an assurance to the principal. "I'll take care of the problem myself."

It was a bold claim. Like the pillow she was mending, her family was coming apart at the seams.

The void Cameron Wade had left in their lives was large enough to qualify as a black hole. Unwittingly, in the course of a couple of weeks, Patricia had let herself come to depend on him. Suddenly all the little things he had done to help out stood out in high relief in a

collage of chaos. In addition to resuming the work of
two or three able-bodied adults, Patricia found herself
constantly cast in the role of a referee. Since she had
banned Cameron from the house, the children were out
of sorts with her, with each other and with the world in
general.

Even little Amy, who by all rights should have been
too young to understand the tensions straining her
mother's usual good nature, seemed to be acting out of
pure spite. Just this morning she threw her favorite
breakfast on the floor, refusing to eat a single bite, resisted her afternoon nap and tossed her favorite doll in
the toilet. Luckily Patricia caught her before she could
flush.

All in all, life post-Cameron was turning into one
long, trying ordeal. Patricia tied a double knot in the
thread, bit it off between her teeth, and surveyed her
handiwork.

"As good as new," she said to herself, studying the
axiom stitched there about a home being made not of
walls and beams but of love and dreams. A fat tear fell
upon the needlepoint and blurred her vision.

Dreams were, after all, illusive things. Her dream of
someday becoming Cameron's wife was destroyed by
a cruel ruse. The knowledge that any tenderness toward
her had come not from his heart but from greedy ulterior
motives was more than she could bear. She wasn't sure
when exactly she had fallen in love with the rogue.
Perhaps the day she had fallen off a ladder and into his
strong arms. Maybe the day he had covered the boys'
emu-roping shenanigans with that pathetic fib to protect
them. Or when he offered up his antique watch as a
teething ring. Or the first time he kissed her and made
her forget everything outside of her own tingly skin.

Patricia knew only that she loved him with all her heart. She also understood that unfortunately, like her father, Cameron's attachment to her was a conditional thing.

Her thumb firmly ensconced in her mouth, Amy climbed up on the couch beside Patricia.

"Where's Da-Da?" she demanded to know.

The knowledge that Amy was asking not for the father she did not know but for Cameron made Patricia break down and cry. If only her heart could be mended as easily as the pillow which caught the flow of her tears!

"I don't know, honey. I just don't know."

Cameron looked at the check in his hands and shook his head in disbelief. It had to be a mistake. Never in his wildest dreams had he envisioned so many zeroes strung together.

His dreams. Those grand, foolish beasts had consumed the last two decades of his life. Now they roared at the outrageous fortune which Cameron presented to them. In the echo of their laughter, the fickle creatures made a mockery of his wretchedness.

He had everything he'd ever wanted. And at the same time he had nothing.

His face and name were destined to be splashed on billboards and advertisements across the nation, but the man who was to be touted as a hero was feeling anything but heroic. He gestured for the bartender to bring him another beer. Funny how in his moment of triumph there was nobody to celebrate with him. His victory was as hollow and empty as the chambers of his heart.

Studying the amber-colored brew the bartender set before him, Cameron contemplated a lifetime of trying to "get back" at the world, while real heroes went about the business of making the world a better place to be, in quiet, unobtrusive ways. Heroes like a certain single mother internally driven by integrity, a sense of who she was, and what was best for her children. In Cameron's book that was far more valiant than some big-shot cowboy who mistakenly thought he could settle a score with fate with a pile of dough and a big, shiny belt buckle.

The bartender had a smile as big as a crescent moon plastered on his face. "This one's on the house," he said. After all, it wasn't every day that a championship bull rider bellied up to his bar. "I hear you're well on your way to being a millionaire, Mr. Wade. Congratulations."

Cameron cringed at the man's formality. The last time anyone had addressed him as Mr. Wade had been when Patricia had threatened to sue him if he backed out of the contract he'd been in such a hurry to sign. The memory brought a wry smile to his lips. The lady had more spunk than she knew what to do with. She'd certainly surprised the heck out of him the other night when she'd thrown his offer to buy her out back in his face.

It had been the foolish act of a proud woman.

With back taxes owed against the place, Cameron knew it was only a matter of time before she would be forced into bankruptcy. The thought of Patricia and the children losing their home to the bank soured his stomach. He pushed the half-empty beer away from him, wishing it was as easy to set aside the haunting images of what was to happen to the family he had come to love despite himself. In his mind's eye, he could clearly see Johnny, Kirk and little Amy all bundled up in the car, peering out the back window as their mother pulled away from a home that no longer belonged to them.

Peeling off the label on his bottle, Cameron considered the silver flakes left on his fingertips. Where would they go, he wondered. Patricia had never mentioned any other family who might be willing to help her out. She had spoken to him a little of the domineering father who actually wanted to see his daughter fail. The one who would relish the sight of her crawling back to beg his forgiveness.

Perhaps she would be forced to turn to some other man less bullheaded than a fool cowboy set more on his own desires than on her happiness. A flash of intense jealousy jarred him from his seat. Would that lucky someone be able to arouse her passions as he had? Would he treat the children well?

The bartender looked brokenhearted as Cameron rose to go.

"If ya don't mind my askin', what're ya gonna do with all your money?" the fellow inquired, wiping his hands on his apron. "Is it true you're thinking of breaking the very bank that broke your old man?"

Eager to be away from such fawning fools, Cameron slapped a tip down on the polished counter. "I do mind your asking. I mind it very much."

As he crossed the street and entered the very bank that had called in the loan on the Wade property almost two decades ago, every eye in the bar followed Cameron's loose-legged gait.

In a small town, it's easy to watch life circle back upon itself. An old man in the corner alluded to it when he said, "What goes around, comes around, I always say."

* * *

"Who could that be at this time of day?" Patricia muttered to herself.

The knock at the front door was as insistent as the headache that had plagued her all day. Johnny didn't give her a chance to find out for herself. He darted past her and threw open the door.

"Cameron!"

At the pronouncement, Kirk came running, almost toppling his mother who stood transfixed in the entryway. By the time she could snap her mouth shut, both boys were wrapped around their visitor's legs so tightly he couldn't move. Never one to be left out of the excitement, Amy pushed her way through her mother's legs, demanding that Cameron pick her up.

As much as he would have liked to oblige, his hands were full. Juggling the biggest bouquet of roses Patricia had ever seen, Cameron struggled to keep his balance. He peeked sheepishly out from behind the fragrant blooms and asked, "Would you mind taking these from me?"

Patricia thought his voice as rich and warm as brandy on a cold winter's day. She eyed him suspiciously before taking pity on him. Once he was freed from his fragrant burden, the children resumed their attack. Never had Patricia seen them give anyone such warm, welcoming bear hugs.

"We've missed you!" they cried out.

"I've missed you, too," Cameron replied, ruffling their hair and tossing Amy up in the air and catching her the way she had come to expect. He set the gleeful tot down before looking into Patricia's eyes and inquiring. "Do you mind if I come in for a minute?"

She hesitated, and Cameron could see her struggle

with emotions that threatened to destroy any chance he might have.

"Please," he said so softly that a less sensitive woman would not have noticed the effort the word cost him.

Not waiting for their mother's permission, the children dragged him into the living room, demanding to know where he'd been. Until he stepped back inside this house, Cameron hadn't realized how much he had missed the clutter. Signs of life and love were strewn about in such a haphazard fashion that one might miss their importance unless distance and longing had been able to put them in their proper perspective.

"The flowers are lovely," Patricia said stiffly. It hurt to see her children clinging to this man with the obvious intention of never letting him go.

"And there's something else that I want you to have," Cameron said, taking an envelope out of his coat pocket.

She took it from him, opened it, and read it.

Once. Twice. Three times over.

"I don't understand," she said at last, turning bewildered eyes upon him.

"It's the mortgage on this ranch."

"I can see that," she replied impatiently. "What I want to know is why it's stamped 'Paid in Full.'"

"It's a gift. From me to you. No strings attached."

The look upon Patricia's face was nothing short of incredulous. "Why? Whatever would make you do such a thing?"

Though the answer seemed as obvious as his runaway heartbeat, Cameron did his best to explain. "Because I want you and the children to have what I didn't have when I was growing up. A home no one can ever take away from you. A home for always.''

Tears glistened in Patricia's eyes. She fought to get her words past the lump in her throat. ''You kids need to leave us alone for a minute.''

They looked at her distrustfully. The last time they'd left these two alone, Cameron had gone away without even telling them where he was going or when he was coming back. They were determined not to let that happen again.

''Go on, now,'' Patricia urged. ''There's nothing for you to worry about.''

Feeling untold relief at the assurance himself, Cameron nodded his head in assent, and the children did as they were told. The boys dragged themselves and their little sister from the room without a word of protest.

When they were alone at last, Patricia spoke softly. ''It was sweet of you,'' she began, aware of the breadth of the understatement. ''Incredibly so, but I can't accept your money.''

Cameron placed a finger to her lips. There was no need to put up a brave front for him. He wanted her to know that he understood. She didn't have to explain.

''Really,'' she insisted. ''I appreciate you riding in here like a knight in shining armor to rescue me from the poorhouse, but it truly wasn't necessary.''

Patricia took a deep breath. How could she put into words that which was so hard to understand herself? ''It's important for me to feel like I'm capable of providing for this family on my own. My father would never allow me the freedom to do anything for myself. And Hadley himself needed to be taken care of. Look, Cameron, I just don't want our relationship to be based on financial need, on monetary obligation. If there's going to be any future for us, I have to be a full and equal partner in every way..."

Blood rushed to her face. It wasn't as if he'd ever so much as mentioned marriage. Even if he were interested in pursuing her, it wasn't exactly as if she was coming into such a relationship unfettered. There was that little matter of three rambunctious children to be considered in every decision she was to make.

The grin on Cameron's face could have buttered a Thanksgiving turkey. Hope fluttered foolishly in the pit of his stomach.

Too flustered to go on, Patricia grabbed a check off the fireplace mantel and waved it under his nose. He took it from her. A frown creased his brow as he studied it.

The pride in her voice was unmistakable as she assured him, "It's enough to cover the taxes and keep the bank off my back for a while longer."

"How?"

Happy to satisfy his curiosity, Patricia explained. "I sold a breeding pair. Big Bird and Gertrude McFuzz. I hated to," she admitted, remembering how often he had teased her that she was not raising livestock but expensive pets. "But I felt I had to."

Cameron's laugh was genuine. The admiration in his eyes apparent. He'd had no idea that a pair of emus could bring that kind of money. Maybe he'd have to reconsider his "fowl" feelings for the creatures. Maybe this crazy business wasn't for the birds after all.

"You sure know how to take the wind out of a fellow's sail, don't you?" he asked in chagrin. "Here I was all set to be your hero and you're not even in the market for one."

"Aw," Patricia countered in a soft voice that brought

out the animal in him. "That's where you're wrong,
cowboy. I need a hero just as much as my boys do.
More, if the truth were known. Just because I proved
my independence to myself doesn't necessarily mean
that I want to be alone for the rest of my life."

"It doesn't?" Cameron asked, taking a step toward
her. The light in his eyes burned the distance between
them with the flame of desire.

"No, it doesn't," she repeated in a breathless whisper.

"Then I'd suggest you take a look into that bouquet
and see if there's anything in there you might consider
wearing for the rest of your life."

The world did a crazy loop to loop as Patricia reached
for the flowers. Nestled between red blossoms the size
of her fist was a tiny jewelry box. Inside was a diamond
solitaire, glittering against a blue velvet background.

At the sound of their mother's gasp, the children
raced into the room. There they found Cameron on one
knee asking, "Will you marry me?"

They nodded encouragingly. "Go for it, Mom!"
urged Johnny.

As glad as Cameron was for their support, Patricia
smiled at her children. After all, it was a decision that
affected them all. Still it was she who had the final
word, not they. There was far more to be considered
than her children's approval. Once she had married as
a means of escaping her father's stranglehold. Older
now and wiser, Patricia knew better than to use marriage as a flight from her troubles. And all the money
in the world was not enough for her to ever again endure the kind of marriage she'd had with Hadley—a
one-sided affair in which she felt solely responsible

making it work. She was looking for neither a father figure nor a big, overgrown child.

If she were to marry Cameron, it had to be for love. It had to be because she couldn't bear the thought of living without him. It had to be without any thought to changing his wonderful, stubborn hide.

"Yes," Patricia said, slipping the ring on her finger, knowing that it was never coming off. Cameron would sell his very soul before he would pawn this exquisite token of his love for her.

The children burst into cheers as Patricia threw her arms around Cameron and kissed him with such abandon that she felt him harden behind the worn fly of his jeans.

"Let's set the date for next weekend," he whispered into her ear. "I don't think I can wait any longer than that."

Her eyes shining with anticipation, Patricia nodded in agreement. "All right, but there's something we should get straight before we make any more plans," she said. "Is there some reason that emus and quarter horses can't coexist?"

Cameron rubbed his chin and considered her question thoughtfully. Such an alliance had never occurred to him, but suddenly it didn't seem as ludicrous as he once might have thought.

"No more reason I guess than why some bullheaded cowboy and a crazy Californian transplant can't populate the West with the best of both worlds." He wriggled his eyebrows meaningfully. "Did I mention I'd like to get a start on that populating part right away?" he murmured in a deep, meaningful purr that set every cell in Patricia's body to tingling.

The children giggled uncontrollably and exchanged

playful punches as Cameron gathered Patricia in his arms and kissed her. Long and hard. Hungry and desperate. Such a kiss foretold of a lifetime of tender lovemaking, and promised there was nothing that they could not conquer.

Together.

* * * * *

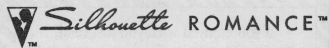

Silhouette ROMANCE™

SOMETIMES THE SMALLEST PACKAGES CAN LEAD TO THE BIGGEST SURPRISES!

Join *Silhouette Romance* as more couples experience the joy only babies can bring!

Bundles of Joy

July 1999
BABIES, RATTLES AND CRIBS... OH MY!
by Leanna Wilson (SR #1378)

His baby girl had suddenly appeared on his doorstep, and Luke Crandall needed daddy lessons—fast! So lovely Sydney Reede agreed to help the befuddled bachelor. But when baby cuddles turned into grown-up kisses, Sydney wondered if what Luke really wanted was *her!*

August 1999
THE BILLIONAIRE AND THE BASSINET
by Suzanne McMinn (SR #1384)

When billionaire Garrett Blakemore set out to find the truth about a possible heir to his family's fortune, he didn't expect to meet a pretty single mom and her adorable baby! But the more time he spent with Lanie Blakemore and her bundle of joy, the more he found himself wanting the role of dad....

And look for more **Bundles of Joy** titles in late 1999:

THE BABY BOND by Lilian Darcy (SR #1390)
in September 1999

BABY, YOU'RE MINE by Lindsay Longford (SR #1396)
in October 1999

Available at your favorite retail outlet.

Silhouette®

If you enjoyed what you just read,
then we've got an offer you can't resist!

Take 2 bestselling love stories FREE!

Plus get a FREE surprise gift!

Clip this page and mail it to Silhouette Reader Service™

IN U.S.A.	**IN CANADA**
3010 Walden Ave.	P.O. Box 609
P.O. Box 1867	Fort Erie, Ontario
Buffalo, N.Y. 14240-1867	L2A 5X3

YES! Please send me 2 free Silhouette Romance® novels and my free surprise gift. Then send me 6 brand-new novels every month, which I will receive months before they're available in stores. In the U.S.A., bill me at the bargain price of $2.90 plus 25¢ delivery per book and applicable sales tax, if any*. In Canada, bill me at the bargain price of $3.25 plus 25¢ delivery per book and applicable taxes**. That's the complete price and a savings of over 10% off the cover prices—what a great deal! I understand that accepting the 2 free books and gift places me under no obligation ever to buy any books. I can always return a shipment and cancel at any time. Even if I never buy another book from Silhouette, the 2 free books and gift are mine to keep forever. So why not take us up on our invitation. You'll be glad you did!

215 SEN CNE7
315 SEN CNE9

Name	(PLEASE PRINT)	
Address	Apt.#	
City	State/Prov.	Zip/Postal Code

* Terms and prices subject to change without notice. Sales tax applicable in N.Y.
** Canadian residents will be charged applicable provincial taxes and GST.
   All orders subject to approval. Offer limited to one per household.
   ® are registered trademarks of Harlequin Enterprises Limited.

SROM99   ©1998 Harlequin Enterprises Limited

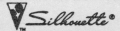

THE MACGREGORS OF OLD...

#1 *New York Times* bestselling author

NORA ROBERTS

has won readers' hearts with her enormously popular MacGregor family saga. Now read about the MacGregors' proud and passionate Scottish forebears in this romantic, tempestuous tale set against the bloody background of the historic battle of Culloden.

Coming in July 1999

REBELLION

One look at the ravishing red-haired beauty and Brigham Langston was captivated. But though Serena MacGregor had the face of an angel, she was a wildcat who spurned his advances with a rapier-sharp tongue. To hot-tempered Serena, Brigham was just another Englishman to be despised. But in the arms of the dashing and dangerous English lord, the proud Scottish beauty felt her hatred melting with the heat of their passion.

Available at your favorite retail outlet.

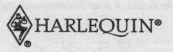

HARLEQUIN®

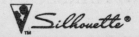